MORTAL SINS

The Second Matthew Grace Casebook

JOHN L. FRENCH

PADWOLF
PUBLISHING

PADWOLF PUBLISHING INC.
WWW.PADWOLF.COM
www.facebook.com/Padwolf

THE MAGIC OF SIMION TOMBS
© 2021 John L. French

cover by Patrick Thomas

Publishing History and Notes
"The Mark of Cain" was first originally published as "Cain" and first appeared in Strange Worlds 8, January 2001, Wild Cat Books.
All other stories are original to this volume.

Buzz McHale, Don Morris, Gardner Investigations, Joseph Mazzano, and William (Bill) Scott were created by Patrick Thomas a
nd first appeared in The Assassin's Ball
by Patrick Thomas and John L. French, Gray Rabbit Press, 2014

ISBN 978-1-890096-93-9
FIrst Printing.

When I was a Crime Scene Supervisor for the Baltimore Police Crime Scene Unit, she was my friend, my right hand, and, when I needed it, my conscience.

For all her help, advice, and guidance, this book is dedicated to:

Carolyn Chambers

CONTENTS

BACK IN THE GAME

Emma Mae Summers was sitting in her living room watching the latest season of Runway Models when three men kicked in her front door. They took turns beating her and, when they were done, they dragged her out to the middle of Fremont Avenue where one of them emptied most of a 9mm clip into her body. He saved the remaining bullets for her face, denying her loved ones the cold comfort of an open coffin at her funeral.

No one called 9-1-1 for Emma Mae, not until it was over. And while most of the block had watched her die, when the police came no one spoke up for her. In Baltimore, there's no future in being a witness to a crime. Just ask Emma Mae. She had been one.

Emma Mae's death was the lead story on the nightly news. Not that senseless violence on a Baltimore street is news anymore. It's more of a daily occurrence. But leading with a murder keeps people from switching to a basic cable cooking show or another rerun of Law & Order.

Which is what I was about to do when my phone rang. It was my supervisor. The conversation started with me saying "Hi, Sharon" and her saying "Matthew, I need you on Fremont Avenue" and me ending with "I'm on my way."

"I thought you didn't do that anymore," my wife Linda said after I hung up.

I didn't. My position as head of the Forensic Investigation Unit of the State's Attorney's Office was supposed to be 8-4, Monday to Friday. But, as I explained to Linda, this was special. What I didn't say was that since giving up my job as a CSI and then as a private investigator there was a part of me that wanted, maybe needed, to be out in the field again.

"Well, I won't wait up. Have fun." Then she kissed me in a way that made me regret having to go out alone on a cold November night instead of going to a nice, warm bed with the woman I love.

It wasn't raining, but it was the kind of a night where it might at any moment. When I pulled up at the end of Fremont I tried to remember the last time I had been on a crime scene. Years ago, just before I took the SAO job. But as I got out of my car and walked toward the yellow tape it all came back to me and it seemed like yesterday.

I stopped at the tape, fighting the urge to lift it and duck under like I had so many times before. But this wasn't my scene. I was a visitor here, and so I waited for a uniform to come over.

"Yes?" she asked.

"State's Attorney's Office." I flashed my ID. She did not seem impressed.

"So?"

"So ask Parker to come over."

"What makes you think he's here?"

"It's a homicide scene, where else would he be? Besides, I can see him from here. Tell him it's Grace."

The officer went over to a man looking down at a sheet-covered body. He turned in my direction then, shaking his head, walked my way.

Joshua Parker was a big, black, bear of a man. The heavy coat and fedora he wore against the unseasonable cold and impending rain made him seem even bigger. For a moment I flashed back to my first major case as a Baltimore CSI, with Parker curtly telling me to "Look for clues, Grace. That's what you're being paid for." His stopping on his side of the tape brought me back to now.

No greeting. No "How are you doing?" Not even a "What are you doing here?" Just a growled, "Did She send you?"

"She" was Celina Alston, the State's Attorney for Baltimore City. Alston was so hated by the members of the BPD that they refused to even mention her name. "She" and "The State's Attorney" were the only printable things they called her. It had been like that since she tried to put several members of the BPD in jail following an in-custody death then put another one in prison for murder.

I shook my head. "Sharon Manchester sent me."

Parker nodded. "Manchester's one of the good ones." Hers was a name he would say. He lifted the tape and bade me enter.

"I don't have to tell you not to touch anything."

My hands were in my pockets, and not just because they were cold. "I still remember, Deacon," I said, using an old nickname that no one but me had ever dared call him to his face. I did it to remind him of all he and I had been through, both good and bad. Not that he would have forgotten. He was the one who got me the job with the SAO. It was either that or throw me in jail.

We stopped short of Emma Mae's body. Parker gave me time to read the scene if I was still able. It turned out that I was.

From where I was standing I could see the forced front door. There were bloody streaks from her hopefully unconscious body having been dragged to the street. Around her covered form were over a dozen cartridge cases. And I knew that once the Medical Examiner removed her body there would be bullets in the bloody mess left behind. I was glad I would not have to be the one to search through it to find them.

Flashes of light came from inside the house. The crime scene technician taking pictures. Over to the side, there was another tech waiting for the scene to clear so he could do a 360° scan of the area. Lots of changes since I had worked a scene. I'm told that they'll soon have drones for aerial photos.

"You need to go in?" Parker asked, nodding toward the house.

I didn't want to but I knew I should so I could give Sharon a full picture later that day. "Yeah," was all I said. We stepped back to wait while the crime scene people finished their job.

Emma Mae's living room was nothing I hadn't seen hundreds of times as a crime scene tech. A nicely kept room filled with photographs and other reminders of a hopefully happy life. Now this room had bloodstains on the floor and walls, the pictures had been knocked over and precious memories shattered.

Looking around, I saw where blood samples had been collected and pieces of whatever had been broken recovered. All the blood would belong to Emma Mae and would only prove useful if the police developed suspects who were too stupid to burn or bleach their clothes.

We left the house and were on the sidewalk when Parker finally asked the question he'd been chewing on since he lifted the tape. "Why, Grace. Why tonight? Why this scene? Was Ms. Summers somebody's aunt or does someone who thinks they're important live in the block?"

"Derek Hobbs," I answered.

"What about him?"

Hobbs wasn't at the top of Baltimore's Most Wanted list but he had made the final five. Drug dealer, gang leader, murder suspect – Hobbs had lots of arrests, so far no convictions.

"Emma Mae Summers saw Hobbs pull the trigger on Preston Walls," I said, just loud enough for only Parker to hear. His "WHAT!" was heard all over the scene.

About three minutes after everyone stopped staring I was in my car driving Parker to Police Headquarters and an interview room in the Homicide Office.

"Now what's this about Emma Mae Summers being a witness in the Walls murder and why weren't we told?"

Even when you know you haven't done anything wrong, when you know that at any time you can get up and leave, there's something intimidating about being in a police interview room. That's the whole idea. Rooms like that are made to be intimidating. Especially when the person across the table from you is a homicide lieutenant whose last word to you was a shouted "WHAT!" and is right now doing his best to keep his anger under control.

I knew he wasn't mad at me, not yet anyway, but rather at the people I work for. But they weren't alone in the room with him and I was. For a moment, I thought about being my old smart-ass self to see how mad I could get him but decided it was neither the time nor the place. Instead, I went with the truth.

"I didn't know until Sharon told me …" I checked my watch.

It was well after midnight. "… last night. The SAO was playing this one close. Miss Summers called Sharon's office right after the shooting. Sharon had represented her nephew back when she was a defense attorney. Miss Summers told her that she had heard the shots and looked out her window. She didn't know Walls but Hobbs grew up in her neighborhood and was standing under a streetlight when he put the last two into him. Sharon took it right to She Who Is Not to Be Named. Miss Summers's name never left the SAO. Unlike the last three witnesses."

Over the last six months, three other witnesses had been killed – Darren Alvarez, Jesse McLeod, Danielle Hyde. Three unrelated homicides. Three witnesses whose names were known only to God, the SAO, and select members of the BPD. And three public murders right before their Grand Jury testimony.

Parker thought about this for a minute. "She didn't trust us."

"She's never trusted you."

"And you didn't know." It was more of a statement than a question but Parker was murder police. They always asked the same question more than once and waited for different answers.

"Maybe She was afraid that I'd tell my favorite homicide lieutenant."

"And who might that be?" The rare joke from Parker was followed by, "And now she's got a problem."

"Right. If it wasn't the cops and it wasn't God, whoever leaked Emma Mae's name worked for the State's Attorney."

"Which means, Grace, that you have a problem. Or soon will."

Parker gave me his biggest smile and held it until the "Oh crap" moment hit and I figured it out.

My fears were confirmed about 10 a.m. when Sharon called me into her office. "Well?" she asked.

I gave her a verbal summary along with a paper copy of the report I had just emailed to her. Like many of the more experienced people at the SAO, Sharon preferred hardcopy to PDF. (And by "experienced" I meant old, or rather older. The younger Assistant State's Attorneys don't share this prejudice.)

"Damn," she said when I finished. She followed that up with, "It's inhouse, isn't it, Matthew? Someone in this office is leaking information."

"Someone is selling information," I corrected. Before she could ask I explained. "Four murders, four unrelated cases. And who knows how many other witnesses warned off rather than killed."

Sharon shook her head. "Leaking, selling, doesn't really matter, does it? What does matter is that we find the person or persons who are doing it. If that woman on Channel 11 finds out about this …"

"Alston won't be able to blame the police like she did the last few times."

Sharon didn't like my comment but didn't disagree with me. Instead, she said, "The problem is that thanks to cloud-based information storage and shared drives, too many people have access to sensitive information. There's almost no one to trust."

I knew what was coming.

"Except you."

And there it was.

"What makes you think you can trust me?" It was a valid question. My past was filled with questionable actions and old sins committed in what I thought was the name of justice. Some of these I regret, but only some.

"Matthew, your job is looking over reports from the BPD's Crime Lab, making sure they're complete and suggesting further action. The names you see belong to victims and suspects and I'm willing to bet that you don't pay attention to any of them."

She was right. When I was a crime scene tech I remembered the crime scenes and not the people who were hurt on them. Now when I review reports I'm looking at photographs taken, sketches drawn, and if analyses and comparisons have led to any identifications.

"Plus you were a private investigator for a time, and a good one." She should know. When Sharon was a defense attorney I worked both for her and against her. "I talked it over with Celina and we both agree that you're the perfect one to undertake this investigation."

"Do I get a choice?"

"Only if you have another job lined up."
"Then I accept."

In some cases, you follow the suspects. In others, you follow the money. Me, I started out following the case files – who had them, where were they stored, how were they viewed. I was given full access to emails, drives, and databases. This was only after I tried to gain access on my own.

As using the computer at my workstation wasn't a fair test, I tried to hack the system from home. I still had intrusion software from my PI days and had kept it updated and added more because, well, you never know when you might be given your last paycheck and escorted from the building carrying the cardboard box of shame. I've kept up my PI license for the same reason.

To say my efforts were a complete failure would not be accurate. I did get into the system and managed to knock on some doors and ring some bells but never made entry. I also didn't get caught which was a nice consolation prize.

So I turned to Webster. Webster was a hacker who had unofficially aided Grace Investigations back in the day. I used him when a system was too hard for me to crack or when I needed a certain level of plausible deniability.

"Are you sure this is legal?" Webster asked after I tracked him down and explained what I needed.

"It's okay. I'm authorized."

"That's what you said the last time."

"We didn't get caught, did we?"

"Yes, we did."

"Well, we didn't go to jail."

"Only because I found the pictures of the congressman with the senator's wife. Really, if people are going to take those kinds of photos they need to use a real camera and not their phones."

I steered him back on topic and watched as he had about as much luck as I had.

Which was what I had been hoping for. With the SAO's systems not vulnerable to outside intrusion, the pool of suspects was now limited to those who worked the cases.

That's when the "virus" hit the SOA computers. At least, that was the cover story. Over the next week the laptops, desktops, and other issued equipment belonging to certain members of the SAO were taken and later returned to their users. To be fair, Webster and his merry gang of cyber privateers did do extensive virus scans. They even found a few that had gotten past the city's lowest bidder protective software. They also found unauthorized music and video files, two clerks running an online dating service for legal professionals, and one very nasty Assistant State's Attorney with some very nasty NSFW photographs. What they didn't find were any emails, texts, or unprotected documents relating to the dead witnesses, the murdered victims, or the defendants arrested for the murders. Neither was there anything other than normal correspondence among the ASA's, law clerks, and investigators working those cases.

That told me a few things. However the information was leaving the building, it wasn't electronically. It was being done old-style – word of mouth, telephone, or hardcopy. Also, there had to be a common thread linking all the cases. And that meant that I could start annoying people in the name of justice.

Annoy them I did. Without any explanation other than "Alston's orders" and a shrug, I followed people around, watched them work, and kept track of how they handled the voluminous amount of hardcopy documents generated in this supposedly paperless workplace. I watched these documents being read, filed, or put into the shredder bins after they had been scanned or were no longer needed. It was boring, easy work and a part of me enjoyed meeting people, listening to their gripes and complaints, and hearing how they would change things if only they were in charge.

But there was another part of me that was very aware that at any time another brave soul who had defied the "Stop Snitching" culture that was a part of Baltimore's dark side might be dragged out on to the street and shot to death as a warning to others. And if that happened, part of the blame for that person's death would be on me for not being smart enough to figure out how the information was leaving the building.

Back when I worked crime scenes, it was me against whoever had committed the crime. They had left something behind or taken something away and I had to discover what it was. A burglar had broken into a house and I had to find the point and method of entry. There was a hit-and-run and I had to come up with a description of the car from the debris left on the scene. When I was a PI it was me against the client's target. They were stealing and I had to figure out how. They were cheating and I had to find out where and with whom. They had a secret and I had to uncover it. It was all a game to me, a game I was good at, a game I hadn't played since I took the job with the SAO and started pushing paper.

I holed up in my office and started to think about this game. Its objective, its rules, the moves my unknown opponent might make and how I could counter them.

The rules mostly didn't matter. The objective was to win. When it came to the moves, well, to figure out a magician's trick don't ask how they did it, ask how you would do it. It was only when I remembered this that I knew I had been away from the game too long. But now that I was back in it, I'd be damned if I was going to lose the first match.

I thought about how I would get information out of the SAO building. Computers could be monitored. Talking to the bad guys, either on a landline or on a personal or burner cell – not a good idea. Who knows who's monitoring them? Face to face, someone might be watching.

So it's by paper. And since it involved unrelated cases I'd need an organization. (Which some would argue would eliminate most city agencies.) And I'd have to be able to get the documents out of the building without being noticed or even suspected.

Then it hit me. It was Chesterton's Invisible Man. It was Burke's Mr. Ottermole. It was the Purloined Letter. It was one of those things everyone sees but nobody notices. I knew how it was being done. The only problem was that to prove it I had to set someone up to be killed.

The witness was one Eric "Magik" Douglas, a mid-level dealer who was up on charges and just happened to be in the right place at the right time. He had watched Emma Mae get dragged out of her house and knew two of the three men who had killed her. In exchange for a walk, a new ID, and an apartment out of state, he was willing to tell a grand jury who these men were.

After Magik sang to the Grand Jury, his song could not be unsung. If he were shot down leaving the Mitchell Courthouse his testimony would still be admissible. There was no one to threaten; he loved no one and no one loved him. He only had one brother and Magik had shot him two years ago and had never visited the grave.

A perfect witness. After the indictment would come the search warrants, the arrests, and the deals for the shooters to give up the leak and who was behind it.

After the indictment.

After the Grand Jury.

Which was in two days.

Which is why Joshua Parker and I were sitting in a van on Llewellyn Street waiting for people with bad intent to break into the house where Eric "Magik" Douglas was in hiding.

"This better work, Grace."

"No reason why it shouldn't, Deacon."

"What does She think about it?"

"We'll find out when I tell her."

"Manchester?"

"Same story. Right now, you and the SWAT team are the only ones I trust."

Video and police reports showed what happened in the house. At three a.m. the front door went down. Three armed men came in looking for Magik. Not knowing what he looked like – there was no way they could – they had come prepared to kill anyone in the house who might be him. They weren't expecting the bright lights, they weren't expecting armored people with guns. They weren't expecting to hear, "Police! Move and you're dead."

They didn't move except to carefully put down their pistols

when ordered to do so. No one got dead. The three men were charged with burglary and firearms violations. They were not charged with the attempted murder of Eric "Magik" Douglas or conspiracy to kill him. They couldn't be. Eric "Magik" Douglas did not exist. I had made him up.

"So let me get this straight," Sharon Manchester said the next day. "The information was going out in the shredder bins?"

I nodded. "It was the only way. Documents go in the bin. Charm City Shred-It picks up the bins to shred what's inside. Everyone here forgets about them. Except that the ones who work for Charm City Shred-It didn't shred anything until they looked it over. Then they'd sell whatever info they found to whoever needed it the most."

"So you …"

"Created Magik Douglas and gave him a story. Then I did the paperwork, which I put in a shredder bin the day before they were due to be picked up. I notified Parker and his people did the rest."

"Why not tell Celina?" The look I gave Sharon was all the answer she needed. "And why not me?"
"Plausible deniability."

"Which means you didn't trust me either." I didn't deny it. She's my supervisor and my friend but Sharon is still a lawyer.

"So all this for a burglary rap and handgun violations?"

I handed her the report I had just received from Parker. "And murder. One of the three was carrying the same gun used to kill Emma Mae Summers. The guns of the other two also had murders on them. They'll soon start singing and then we'll know who in Charm City Shred-It was behind it all. They'll give us the names of the other shooters."

I didn't understand the look I got along with Sharon's "Good job, Matthew" until later. The burglary charges were dropped in favor of guilty pleas for Emma Mae's and the other murders. The shooters gave up Derek Hobbs as part of the deal. He pled out as well. There was no testimony, no public statement about the involvement of Charm City Shred-It. No one from the company was charged. The murders of the other witnesses went unsolved.

I asked why. No one answered so I kept asking until I was told to drop it. I kept quiet but kept digging. I found out that Charm City Shred-It was a local company owned by Leslie Resnick. Ms. Resnick was also local – born, raised, and educated in Baltimore all the way through college and law school. She dropped out of the University of Baltimore in her second year but not before making friends with Celina Alston.

That I had missed that, that I didn't see it coming was another reminder of how long I'd been out of the game. Well, I'm back in it now.

PLAYING THE ANGLES

In many ways, it was a typical Baltimore murder. One man shoots another man. A third man gives chase. More shots are fired. In the end, there are two wounded and one dead. Just another day in Charm City and the lead-in to the evening news.

Officer Dana Hays was on foot patrol in the Western District when he heard the sound of gunfire. Running toward it, he saw one man in the street and another running away.

Hays was new, just a year out of the Academy. In the excitement of coming up on an on-view shooting, he forgot his primary responsibility of seeing to the wellbeing of the victim and instead, with an ultimately useless cry of "Stop! Police!" he gave chase.

The chase led Officer Hays down the street then into an alley. Due to his lack of familiarity with the sector, he did not know that the alley let out on a vacant lot.

The lot was the result of the corner house on that block of Mulberry Street having been partly torn down. When Officer Hays emerged from the alley there was a muralled wall to his right and part of a brick wall in front of him. As he turned toward Stricker Street, Officer Hays found that man he had been chasing was waiting for him.

Hays had his service weapon out but hesitated to bring it up. The shooter, later identified as Melvin McCabe, did not hesitate. Bringing up his own pistol, McCabe fired five times.

Hays caught the first bullet in his chest. His body armor stopped it but he still felt the impact. Then there was pain in his right leg and left arm as bullets entered and passed through both of them.

Hays almost went down, almost gave in to the pain and collapsed. But he believed that if he did, the shooter would come close enough to finish the job and there would be no one there to stop him if he did. This was Baltimore, and people in Baltimore did not like or trust cops.

Bracing himself against the mural, struggling to remain upright, Officer Hays fought through the pain. Looking toward Stricker Street, he saw a smiling man pointing a gun in his direction. Bringing up his Smith and Wesson, Officer Hays returned fire.

His target ran away. Unable to pursue, Hays slumped against the wall, hoping that backup was coming.

Then came the screams and the wailing. Someone shouted, "That cop killed Angel." A mother cried out, "My baby's dead."

Officer Hays looked toward the screams and the moans. He stumbled forward several feet and saw a small form lying on the corner.

No, he thought. *I didn't, I couldn't. I killed a kid.*

News that a police officer had gunned down a child spread quickly. A crowd formed. While some stood vigil over Angel's body, the rest headed toward Officer Hays with anger in their hearts and vengeance on their minds.

It was every cop's nightmare and Officer Hays was living it. An innocent dead by his hand. Believing himself guilty, Hays dropped his gun, fell to his knees, and gave himself over to the judgment of the crowd.

It was later said by some who were there that that action saved Hays's life. As angry as they were, those in the crowd were mostly decent, God-fearing people and had no taste for harming a defenseless man, even one who had shot down their Angel. Several of the older men circled Officer Hays, protecting him from the hate and vengeance of the younger ones.

Police units finally arrived, first patrol cars with uniformed officers, then unmarked cars with detectives. The scene was secured, the crowd moved behind yellow barrier tape, the Crime Scene Unit was called. Bending the rules in the interests of peace and the mood of the crowd, Angel's uncle, a Baptist minister, was allowed to stay by her body while detectives gathered information and the Crime Lab processed the scene.

Darren Boyd, the original victim, the one with whom Officer Hays did not remain, had driven himself to Sinai Hospital where he was treated and released. Melvin McCabe got away, at least for a time.

Had all this happened a decade or more ago, the death of Angel Collins would have been handled as a tragic, unfortunate accident. But Angel was killed during a time of unrest, when the actions and attitudes of law enforcement toward minorities were under increased scrutiny and criticism. Cell phone videos captured abuses that in the past would have been glossed over and more and more police officers were being held accountable for their behavior by society and the courts. The watchmen were being watched and judgments were being handed down.

Two years before the death of Angel Collins, five officers were indicted for the in-custody death of Ollie Wallace, a known drug user and burglar who had been caught breaking into a store. What happened on that scene was never fully explained, either by the evidence or by the officers. The Medical Examiner found drugs in Wallace's system along with blunt force trauma to his body. Ultimately, Wallace's death was ruled a homicide.

There were protests, demonstrations, and riots both before the officers' indictments and after their acquittal by a judge in a bench trial. Each time there was massive property damage. Pharmacies were looted for drugs and stores for their merchandise. There were hundreds of arrests, countless officers and civilians injured, and several deaths. Now, with Angel's death, it appeared that Baltimore would once again erupt in righteous anger.

Officer Hays's injuries were not life-threatening. Both wounds were through and through but they were serious enough to require a hospital stay and therapy later.

When his sources at Shock Trauma let him know that Hays had been admitted, against all procedure Homicide Lieutenant Joshua Parker chased everyone out of the young cop's hospital room then blocked the door so no one could enter. He did not want the young man to talk to Internal Affairs, his FOP representative, or the detectives who caught the case. He definitely did not want him talking to whomever the State's Attorney sent over. Hays was full of guilt, blaming himself for the death of a little girl. Parker did not know if he was right to do so, but that's not the sort of statement anyone would want to make in front of someone who was going to write it down and put it in a report.

With Hays in his bed and Parker at his side, the lieutenant said, "Listen up, Officer," in the no-nonsense voice of God tone he developed shortly after he had made sergeant and had refined and improved upon over the following twenty years. "I have not read you your rights. Your lawyer's not here. Your rep's not here. Your mother is not here. But as soon as your doctors say they can, there is going to be a whole raft of people coming in here who do not have your best interests at heart. Tonight will probably be your last moment of peace so I think you should reflect on what happened and decide what you want to tell them and who you want with you when you do. Now I know most of the doctors and more importantly the nurses in here and I'll ask them to keep the wolves at bay for as long as they can. But sooner or later they're going to come in."

"I appreciate that. Thanks, Lieutenant."

"Just two things, Hays."

"What's that, Sir?"

"First, what the hell were you thinking when you left a bleeding victim lying on the street? Don't answer that. You weren't thinking. And to my mind, the smartest thing you did today was to drop your weapon and give yourself to the crowd. It probably saved your life."

"I wish it hadn't."

"I don't. That would have been a messy scene to investigate and an even messier one to prosecute." Parker got up. "You think about things. I'll give you all the time I can."

Before Parker could leave, Hays said, "Lieutenant, we've never met but I've heard about you. Is it true you never lie?"

Parker nodded. "Mostly. Why?"

"What's going to happen? Not to me, but to the city?"

Sighing deeply, Parker sat back down. "When Ollie Wallace died stores burned, otherwise good people did bad things and got locked up, other people were hurt or killed. And Ollie Wallace was a thieving, robbing, drug-using sinner who may or may not have been killed by the police. Angel Collins was a beautiful little girl who was shot down by a cop. Son, what do you think is going to happen? The last time, this city went to Hell. This time, it's going all the way to the Ninth Circle."

"Arrest me, Lieutenant."

For all the years I've worked with, and sometimes against, Joshua Parker, I've never known him to be surprised. When he told me about this later, he confessed that that night he was. He said he just stared at Officer Hays for a moment, then asked,

"What? Are you sure? Hays, think about this before …"

"Lieutenant, it's not the drugs talking. The IV is for fluids and the doctors told me that my pain meds are non-narcotic. I have the right to remain silent. I have the right to an attorney. I know my rights and I waive them. I left a man bleeding in the street. After I was wounded the pain was such that I was not thinking clearly and I discharged my weapon without making sure I had a clear target. I'm sure as Hell guilty of something. So, arrest me."

"Again, Hays, are you sure? What they'll do to you …"

"Lieutenant, about a year ago I stood on a stage and swore to risk my life to protect this city. I guess I can risk my freedom to do the same."

What Officer Hays proposed made sense – one man for the sake of the city. It was, in a way, the basis of the religion Deacon Joshua Parker preached on Sundays when he could. But Parker was not about to make the decision. He called Police Commissioner McHale's personal cell.

"Joshua, this better be important. There's an angry mob growing at Mulberry and Stricker and it looks like it's going to break loose and come our way. Plus, there are protests that are forming where Ollie Wallace went down and at several other sites where there was a major police-involved incident. The mayor's on the phone to the governor and it looks like we may be under martial law by tomorrow."

"That may not be necessary, Buzz.," Parker told the Commissioner of Hays's offer.

The silence on McHale's end of the phone lasted long enough that Parker thought he had lost the signal. Then …

"Do it," said the Commissioner. "On my order, arrest him for misconduct in office. I'll brief the media. Maybe we can stop this."

News that Dana Hays had been arrested, albeit for something less than murder, calmed the growing crowds. There was some breakage, some looting, but nowhere near as bad as had been feared. There were protests over the next few days, but they were mostly peaceful, with the speakers, however reluctantly, praising the police for doing the right thing – for once. Baltimore breathed a sigh of relief.

At first, Hays's arrest did not sit well with his fellow officers. They saw it as a betrayal, a sacrifice to the mob mentality. When they learned whose idea it was, the debate shifted as to whether Dana Hays was a hero, a fool, or a damned fool. Most agreed that hero or fool, Officer Hays was well and truly damned.

At the worst, everyone expected Hays to be indicted for misconduct in office and probably manslaughter in the death of Angel Collins. But State's Attorney Celina Alston, still smarting from what she saw as a defeat in the case of Ollie Wallace, went for the jugular. Officer Dana Hays was indicted and convicted for depraved-heart murder and sentenced to twenty years in prison.

Two years passed. As Dana Hays served out his sentence in protective custody, Melvin McCabe was arrested when ballistics evidence matched the cartridges cases found on the scene of Dana Hays's shooting to the pistol recovered from McCabe during a drug bust. At his trial, McCabe's attorney used Hays's conviction and argued that his client was only protecting himself from a gun-crazy cop. Despite incontrovertible evidence that he had fired first, a Baltimore jury acquitted McCabe.

Shortly after Melvin McCabe walked out of court a free man, the Maryland Court of Appeals ruled that due to the State's failure to provide full discovery to the defense, improper statements made by the prosecutor during trial, and a juror who failed to disclose that her nephew had been shot by police, Dana Hays's conviction was overturned and he was granted a new trial.

When a convicted person gets a new trial it's like hitting reset on that video game you just can't win. The defense gets to play all over again with a different approach and game plan. When Dana Hays was tried the first time, no one questioned whether or not he fired the bullet that killed Angel Collins. It was assumed and that assumption was not challenged. This time, however, Hays had a new attorney, some guy named William Scott, and that attorney had a new strategy. Yes, Hays was negligent in leaving David Boyd in order to chase Melvin McCabe. And yes, he was reckless in firing his weapon without a clear target. He admitted to both these facts. But he never said, and the State never proved, that any of the bullets he had fired had struck, much less killed, Angel Collins.

Adding to that, due to the volatility of the crowd, the processing of the scene had been a hurried affair. The crime scene investigators had time to photograph the scene, the cartridge cases from Hays's and McCabe's weapons, and the body of Angel Collins, this last done with the child's family and their friends, relations, and neighbors within touching distance and demanding that someone "do something" about the cop who killed their Angel. There was no time to fully and safely document the scene or to search it for additional evidence such as the bullets from Hays's gun, especially the one that hit and passed through Angel.

Which is how I got involved in this whole mess.

I'm Matthew Grace. Once upon a time, I was a crime scene tech. Then I was a PI. Now I'm the head of the State's Attorney's Forensic Investigation Unit. In reality, thanks to budget cuts, I'm the only member of that unit. Normally I push papers – mainly crime scene processing reports and results of comparisons and analyses – from the Crime Lab to the Assistant State's Attorneys. Normally. Today was not a normal day.

I got summoned from the closet that passed for my office to the much larger room where my supervisor, Sharon Manchester, worked. Sharon is a former defense attorney who saw the light after defending a hitman and switched sides. When I walked into her office I knew that something was up. Sharon was standing to one side and her boss, Celina Alston, the State's Attorney for Baltimore City, was sitting behind her desk.

Without being asked I took a seat, wondering what kind of a

mess I was going to be asked, no, told to step into.

"First of all, Mr. Grace, good work on plugging that leak." Before I could say "Thank you" she added, "However, the next time something of that importance comes up I would appreciate my office being kept in the loop."

I had played things close so she had me there. I could have said that I had no way of knowing who to trust and that included her. I could have pointed out that the company responsible for the leak was owned by a friend of hers. But my position in the State's Attorney's Office was an "at will" one and that will belonged to Alston. So, I just smiled and nodded. If she took that as a "Yes, Ma'am" more fool her.

"The Hays case is being retried," Alston said. "As you know, the crime scene was poorly processed, no doubt on orders from the investigating detective. Other than his own words and the testimony of some witnesses who are less than reliable, there is no direct evidence that Hays shot the victim."

"The victim's name was Angel Collins and Dana Hays never said that he shot her."

Alston gave me a look that said she wished she had another option for whatever job she had in mind but I was her only choice. With a terse, "Yes," she went on.

"I want you to go back to Stricker and Mulberry. Use some of that expensive equipment you talked us into buying to scan and recreate the scene. Then show that no one but Hays could have fired the fatal shot."

In other words, cook the scene until I got the results she wanted. I didn't work that way when I was a CSI and I wasn't going to do it then. I was about to tell her that and to hell with "at will" when from behind her I saw Sharon shaking her head. So, I swallowed my questions about possible perjury, this time said, "Yes Ma'am," out loud, and made a hurried exit.

About fifteen minutes later, Sharon came by my office, poked her head in and said, "Matthew, I know you'll do your best." Then, as if to apologize for or at least explain her boss, she added, "This office needs a win."

"So do the Orioles and they have a better manager. Just what is her problem, other than she wants to be mayor and her only campaign strategy is to bash the cops."

Correctly sensing that I was in no mood to talk, Sharon went back to her office. She was right about one thing, I would do my best. I began planning how to do it.

When I started with the SAO, I thought that the position of "Forensic Investigator" would involve some actual investigation. Before I found out how wrong I was, I spent part of the Office's quarter of a billion-dollar budget on some of that "expensive equipment" Alston had mentioned. Included in that purchase was a 360° laser scanner that came with a top-quality digital camera. While I had created some very nice scans of the inside of the Mitchell Courthouse when I was learning how to use my new toys, I had not had occasion to use either in the field. Now I had an excuse.

I drafted an SAO investigator named Cole Williams to stand by me while I did the scans of Mulberry and Stricker. He was a former BPD Robbery detective who, after making his twenty, switched over to the SAO for more money and less work. Like me, he was glad to be doing something other than his regular job, which for him consisted mainly of tracking down witnesses. So that the community would not mistake us for cops out to clear Dana Hays, we both wore jackets with "State's Attorney" prominently displayed on the backs.

Very little of the scene had changed. The mural was still there. As was the brick wall. Even after all this time, there were fresh flowers, balloons, and stuffed animals on the corner where Angel had fallen. One or two sets of marble steps had been replaced with brick and the Formstone had been removed from some houses. Being longtime Baltimore boys, Cole and I agreed that such offenses should be punished by immediate banishment to Howard County and the city of Columbia.

"They probably don't even like Burger Cookies," Cole said as I started setting up the scanner.

"Cole, everybody likes Burger Cookies."

Of course, we drew a crowd of curious onlookers. While I did the scans, Cole went over to the crowd, showed them his SAO badge, and explained what we were doing. When he told them that I was going to be using a laser, some of them backed off further than usual.

It took most of the day to make ten scans. That was probably five more than I needed but I wanted to make sure I had captured all the angles. Each area was documented twice, first by the 360° scanner then by the digital camera linked to the system so as to capture the same area as the scan.

I spent the next two days combining the ten scans into a single cloud-point image then converting that into a RealScene video that would allow anyone with the right software to do a walkthrough of the scene. Then, using the original crime scene photographs, I added the position of Angel's body and what evidence there was to the cloud-point.

The rest should have been easy. Semi-automatic pistols eject cartridge cases to the right. (Which is why you don't hold your Glock sideways because the hot casing might fly into your face.) When he fired, Hays would have been standing to the left of where the casings were found. So all I had to do was draw a line from his position to where Angel Collins had been standing when struck. That would have shown that it was possible, even likely in some people's view, that he had fired the fatal bullet.

Except that that dammed wall was in the way. It was only by a foot or two but the wall was in the way. It wasn't that obvious in the 2D presentation but when I shifted to the 3D version and used Hay's point of view, it was clear that any bullet he might have fired could have not struck Angel. From where he was standing he could not have even seen the corner.

My first thought was that I had done something wrong, positioned Hays too far to the right. I played with the angles, moving Hays's firing position to the left a little at a time. To see the corner, to shoot Angel, he would have had to be too far away for his casings to wind up where they did. I moved him forward. Same answer. The bullets used by the BPD are man-stoppers but aren't powerful enough to go through a brick and cinder block wall.

Maybe it was Angel. Maybe when the bullet struck her she staggered toward the corner. But no, the Medical Examiner's report stated that death was instantaneous and that she would have dropped where she was. Still remembering the number from my crime scene days, I called the ME's Office to make sure. She might have made a few steps, but not the twenty-eight to thirty feet it would have taken for her to be in Hays's line of sight.

After exhausting all possibilities, including taking a good look at the scan of the wall for gaps large enough for a bullet to pass through, I simply sat and stared at my computer screen as I realized the implications of my efforts. Then in English, French, and Latin I mentally cursed the crime scene people for not taking the one photograph that would have shown that not only was Dana Hays not guilty of killing Angel Collins but that someone else had shot the little girl.

Or maybe CSU had taken the photo, and someone had hacked the cloud server on which the pictures were stored and made that photo go away. Part of me told me that I was being paranoid. Another part told me that I was being practical and reminded me of how long I had worked for the BPD and where I was working now and for whom.

Damn it, I thought, *it doesn't matter. The photo wasn't taken or no longer exists.*

I wrote up the report of my findings, copied the RealScene video to DVD, and sent it to Sharon along with a note that I'd see her the next day. Then, after backing up and securing my work, I went home to my wife Linda, looking forward to being with the one person in the world I knew loved me.

The next morning was unusually quiet, for me that is. I had expected a morning summons but none came. There were people running this way and that, and there was that sub-sonic hum that offices get when something big is going on.

I knew what it was and what they were doing. When they released the report, when they dropped the murder charge against Dana Hays, Baltimore would again run riot. The blaze that was forestalled when Hays asked to be arrested would finally flare up, and all I could think about was that while I didn't start the fire, I sure as hell had struck a match.

It was after lunch when I got the summons. Not to Sharon's office but one floor up, the very prestigious office of Celina Alston. When I walked in, she was behind her desk, flanked on one side by her deputy Ogden Manners and on the other by Sharon. The fact that neither of them could look me in the eyes gave me my first clue that I was not going to be congratulated on a job well done.

Alston did look me in the eye. Looking back at her, I saw that she was not pleased. I reflected that given the explosive material I had sent her and which she had on her desk, she had a right not to be. "Don't bother to sit, Mr. Grace," she said, "this won't take long.

"You did a very fine job on this," she said, looking down at my report. "But given that this was done more than two years after the crime and is based on technology not commonly used in court and on what is basically estimates, speculation, and guesswork, this office has decided that we will not be using it in Dana's Hays's retrial."

I was about to object, to say something about there now being a reasonable doubt of Hay's guilt, that there was a possibility that Angel's real murderer was walking free but Alston forestalled me.

"The matter is not open for discussion, Mr. Grace. Now please take Mr. Manners to your office and turn over to him all files, notes, and other material, digital or otherwise, you have on this case. And you are not to discuss this with anyone outside this room. That will be all, Mr. Grace."

I thought about quitting, about threatening to go to William Scott and let him know about the scans and my results. Or better still, drop a line to *The Baltimore Truth*, the city's new daily tabloid.

Then I thought better of it. There were other ways. I thought of a few on the way to my office with Manners.

Neither of us spoke. I had nothing to say. Maybe he was embarrassed by the fact that his boss was so bent on putting cops in prison, or keeping them there, that she had forgotten her oath and the meaning of justice. Or maybe she didn't forget and just didn't care.

When we got to my office, I started handing Manners the files, notebooks, and DVDs that had the Hays case on them. I let him watch as I copied what was on my computer to a thumb drive, delete the original file, then empty my trash bin. Even after I said, "That's it. That's all of it," he had to ask, "Are you sure?" meaning, "Did you just lie to me?"

I stepped into my doorway, giving my office over to him. "Search the place if you like."

Damn if he didn't. He spent a good thirty minutes going through my computer looking for hidden files. He spent another forty on my cloud drives, as if after the data leak a few months ago I'd put anything on them. Maybe he was that stupid but I resented him thinking I was. He picked up some loose CDs and DVDs.

"Blank?" he asked. When I said that they were he fed them into my office shredder.

The last thing Manners did was to open my desk drawers and pocket the loose thumb drives I use to transfer data. No worries there, they were all blank.

"If you're through I need you to sign this," I said when I sensed he was done.

While he was searching I was taking notes. The paper I handed him detailed all the actions he and I had taken. He looked at the paper, decided there was no harm in signing, and scribbled his name.

When I was sure he was gone I took the digital camera off my file cabinet. People think of a camera as something that takes pictures. Most of them don't think of the SD card inside the camera that stores the images. Some of them don't think of the card at all, uploading their photos straight into their computer or, with the newer cameras, right to the cloud. Opening the battery and memory card door, I removed the SD card on which I have saved all my work on the Hays case.

It was almost quitting time so after scanning the receipt I got from Manners and emailing a copy to Sharon I took the rest of the day off. When Linda got home she knew right away something was wrong. I told her what it was.

"I'd tell you to let it go but you're not going to, are you?"

I shook my head. "Never have, never will."

"Which means you're planning to do something foolish."

What can I say? My wife knows me very well. I surprised her by again shaking my head and saying, "Not planning. I did that at work. Tomorrow I start executing. And I'm not doing 'some thing' foolish. I will probably do several foolish things this week."

"Well, if it doesn't work out there's always the security job at the hotel." (Linda is the manager of the Baltimore Albion in Harbor East.) "You can be like Magnum."

"Really, I thought you were joking, or role-playing considering what we did after you brought it up."

When Linda assured me that she had not been joking the only thing left to say was, "Will I have to grow a mustache?"

Running security at one of Charm City's finer hotels was tempting, but before I made any career decisions there were foolish things to do. The next day I called Sharon and told her that I'd be taking a vacation day. She warned me not to do anything stupid and said she'd see me the following day. The next call I asked Linda to make from work. (No, I didn't think the SAO was monitoring my personal phone but there was no sense taking chances.) The call was to the office of Garner Investigations, a small PI firm run by two ex-cops, one of whom was the daughter of the police commissioner. The other just liked to blow things up.

The message wasn't for the Garners. They shared office space and a receptionist with Dana Hays's lawyer, William Scott. Linda left Scott a message to meet someone about the Hays case.

I was sitting in the back booth of a bar called the Pair o'Dice Lounge, one of those neighborhood places that seem to change names and owners every few years. As the Pair o'Dice it seemed to be doing very well. Maybe this one will last.

Scott walked in, looked around, then headed toward my table. I ignored him until he sat opposite me.

"What's this about the Hays's case?" he asked, then he recognized me. "You're Matthew Grace. You work for the State's

Attorney. What the Hell is going on?"

Scott got up to leave. I stopped him with, "Hays didn't kill Angel Collins." When he sat back down I told him why.

"So, they'll be dropping the charges?"

"No, they won't." Again I told him why, adding, "Keep me out of this if you can. Hire your own forensic investigator, you probably know or one or two who do private work. They'll come to the same conclusion I did."

"Or somebody called in an anonymous tip to my office and said they saw you doing the scans. I could summon you. I doubt if you'd commit perjury."

"Don't count on me for anything, Mr. Scott. I was never here and I can prove it."

That should have been one problem solved. Scott's FI would find the same thing I did. The murder case against Hays would be dropped and he'd get time served on the other charges.

Except that the next day *The Baltimore Sun* ran a story about the city turning the vacant lot at Mulberry and Stricker into the Angel Collins Memorial Park and that construction had already begun. The lot had been cleared and a wall taken down.

I had to hand it to Alston. She really wanted a cop's head on a pike to wave around when she ran for mayor. It was going to get messy. Now there was no way Scott was not going to summon me to testify. And if asked on the stand what proof I had of my observations and conclusions, I'd have to tell the jury about the SD card. Then all Hell would break loose. At the least, I'd be fired. At the worst, I'd be charged with theft of SAO property. But that card was now in an envelope taped to the underside of a desk drawer in my office so the charge wouldn't stick since the card had never left the building. Right, and the State's Attorney Office doesn't prosecute innocent cops.

I could go to the media. I could go to the Attorney General. If summoned to testify I could destroy the card the day before I took the stand. Or I could just tell the truth.

By the time I went back to work I knew what to do, what I had to do. I would be Samson among the Philistines. I'd tell Sharon that if murder charges weren't dropped against Hays I'd bring the whole house down. I tried very hard not to think about what happened to Samson when he did that.

Before I could call Sharon, she came to my office. "While you were out, Celina got a call from William Scott. Someone saw you and Cole doing the scans and called his office. He wanted them. Celina told him what she told you, that they were primarily guesswork on your part and that your positional estimates were just that and not evidence. He then said he planned to call you as an expert witness in the area of crime scene processing."

"Damn shame someone took that wall down. Alston could have brought in another expert to prove me wrong."

Sharon ignored me. "You won't be testifying. We made a deal. In the interests of justice and to keep this city from blowing up again, Hays is taking an Alford plea to manslaughter. He'll do two more years then be quietly released."

"It's not right, Sharon."

"No, Matthew, it's not. Hays might be innocent but Baltimore doesn't need more riots. The last two times … do you know how many opioid drugs hit the street after the pharmacies were looted? And there are gangs out there just waiting for it to happen again. Word is that they were good to go when the girl got killed. Only Hays's sacrifice stopped them, and it looks like his plea will stop them again."

"Just one question, Sharon."

"Just one?"

"For now. If Hays didn't shoot Angel, who did?"

She said, "We'll probably never know. Let it go, Matthew." Then she walked away.

I thought Sharon knew me better than that. I was not going to let it go, and I thought I already knew who had shot and killed a little girl. Or rather, I knew how to find out.

In northeast Baltimore County, just before the Harford County line, there's a private care facility that you'd drive by if you didn't know it was there. The quality of care in this place is better than in most hospitals, with very well paid nurses on round-the-clock duty and personal attendants assigned to each resident. It is, of course, very expensive and very exclusive.

One of the residents is a man I call "Mr. Louis." That's not his real name. If I told you what that was you'd probably recognize it. Mr. Louis retired about the same time I started with the State's Attorney's Office. Before that, he was the head of the Baltimore Mob.

Baltimore has lots of criminal gangs. They're mostly drug gangs, but there are also a few biker "clubs," some organized burglary rings, and the scum that deal in human trafficking.

These are not "The Mob." Organized crime in Baltimore stays very low key, preferring that the less organized gangs get the headlines and the jail sentences. Instead, it provides these gangs such services as handshake loans and partnerships, influence with the political and legal systems, and the occasional quiet, never-to-be-seen-again removal of business competitors.

The Mob also runs rackets suck as loan-sharking, union involvement, and high-end escort services. It used to run gambling until the State stepped in with legal lotteries and casinos.

Mr. Louis, associated as he was with certain families in New York, was very successful in running the Baltimore Mob. Some arrests, no convictions, and very little media coverage. It was said that he not only knew where the bodies were buried, but he also had the shovels of those who did the digging and photographs of the burials.

I burned another vacation day and drove out to see him. Why, you might ask, did I have anything to do with a mob boss given the number and seriousness of the crimes he probably committed. Good question.

When I was a PI, Mr. Louis hired me to do a job. It was legal and I did it. After that, I sometimes worked for him and just as often worked against him. I did it in a way that kept us both off Action News at Six, Mr. Louis out of jail, and me out of the trunk of a car in the long term parking lot of Baltimore's Pennsylvania Station. We weren't friends but we respected each other. When I changed jobs and he retired, I made a point of driving up to see him about once a month just to visit. He never asked anything of me, and I never asked anything of him.

That was going to change.

I walked into the facility carrying my usual gifts – a box of Burger Cookies, a big bag of Utz Potato Chips, and a bottle of wine. All the things Mr. Louis's doctors say he shouldn't have. The staff knew what I had in my bag and didn't care as long as nothing set off the metal detector.

When I walked into his suite, Mr. Louis was in a chair in his living room reading a gangster novel. He found them funny. He and I have spent a few afternoons discussing and picking apart novels, TV shows, and movies about crime; me complaining about forensic mistakes and him commenting on how things are really done on the other side.

Looking up from his book, Mr. Louis asked, "So, Mr. Grace, what do you want?"

"What makes you think I want something?"

He shook his head. "You come to see me every four to five weeks, and always on a Saturday. Your last visit was two weeks ago and today is not a weekend."

He was sharp and he had me. "There is something I'd like to discuss."

He could have asked after my wife. He could have told me about his grandchildren and complained that he doesn't see them enough. He could have just said, "Let's talk about something else." If he had, we would have spent the afternoon together after which I would have left with a wasted vacation day and no idea how I was going to get justice for Angel Collins.

Instead, he waved me to a chair and said, "So let's discuss." He already knew about the shooting, the first trial, and the new one. I told him why I thought Dana Hays could not have killed Angel.

"If you're right, Mr. Grace, and except for that one time when you thought you had evidence against me for murder …"

"It was Joe Mozzano."

"Of course it was and, to your credit, you admitted your mistake and fixed things. But other than that, I've never known you to be wrong. So that means someone else killed this little girl.”

I said he was sharp. He probably had already figured it out but it was my story and he let me tell it.

“Someone involved in the west side drug gangs shot Angel to start a riot so that during the looting and violence they could hit and clean out the pharmacies and sell the drugs on the street.”

For a long minute, Mr. Louis thought about what I had said. Finally, “To take advantage of a situation is one thing. To plan for when these situations occur makes sense. To kill a child to provoke such a situation …” He shook his head.

“In my day, I know what we would have done. I know what I would have done.”

He stopped, started thinking again, probably deciding if he should get involved.

“Officer Hays is a good man,” I said. “He made mistakes and he’s paying for them. What’s he’s doing now is for the good of the city, our city.” Mr. Louis started nodding. “You kill a kid to start a riot, what might you do next?”

I shut up. There was nothing more I could say. It was up to Mr. Louis.

“Mozzano runs things now. I think I’ll give him a call, maybe have a discussion with him.”

And that was that. We talked a while longer. Before I left, Mr. Louis made me promise to bring him a cheesecake from Woodlea Bakery. “Bring two, one for the nurses.”

I went back to work. Dana Hays pled out. The city stayed calm. The SD card stayed in the envelope under my desk drawer just in case. At first, every day I expected to hear something. After two weeks I began to think that maybe Mr. Louis didn’t have the influence he once did. I took cold comfort in telling myself that I had done all that I could.

A month after Hays was sentenced a second time for something he didn’t do, a video hit all the media sites and immediately went viral. It was of Felix Lynn, one of Baltimore’s reputed “drug kingpins.” He had several arrests but no convictions. He even once beat a federal RICO charge. He was talking to someone off-camera, and it didn't look like he knew he was being recorded.

"Yeah, that was me, sort of. I got the call from Slow Max about what was going down and I told him to take the shot. He did and made it good. I thought when that girl fell the crowd was going to tear that cop apart. Damn shame he took the weight. We had the pharmacies all picked out. But there'll be other chances."

"Other little girls?" an unseen voice asked.

Lynn shrugged. "If that's what it takes."

Dana Hays was freed within a week. Time served on the lesser charges. When he was released, he thanked God and all those who had believed in him. Some still thought him a hero, others a fool, and there were those who thought that the video was faked. Celina Alston may have been one of them. Her office issued a statement but no apology.

The day after Alston's statement, Sharon called me into her office.

"We might need your testimony after all, Matthew, once Lynn and this Slow Max are found."

"Yeah, damn shame you guys destroyed all my hard work."

"I don't know. Something may have been overlooked and might come up if it's needed for trial." The woman did know me.

Neither my testimony nor the SD card was needed. Slow Max and Lynn were never found. It was as if they'd dropped off the face of the earth, someone said. I doubted that. It was more likely that they were both covered by several feet of earth. As Mr. Louis said, in his day they knew what to do about child killers. They probably still did.

JUSTICE LAID BARE

What is now known as The Mitchell Courthouse was built in 1900. To some, particularly architectural students who wander its hallways and take photographs where they're not supposed to, it's a wonder —marble floors, mosaics, stained glass cupolas, and courtrooms that could be in the movies. Some of them even were. To the public it is impressive. But not to the people who work there.

Too hot in the summer, too cold in the winter, elevators that are more like cats than dogs in that they come when they feel like it, not when they're called. There are no separate meeting rooms for witnesses or lawyers meeting clients. Instead, everyone waits in drafty hallways on uncomfortable benches. Sometimes the family and friends of a murder victim sit opposite the family and friends of the person accused of killing them. It is not a comfortable building. That's why the State's Attorney's Office moved to newer facilities a few blocks south on Baltimore Street.

There is always talk of replacing the Mitchell Courthouse, as well as Courthouse East, its companion building across Calvert Street. But there's no place downtown to construct a new one. One former mayor (the convicted one, not the one currently under indictment) suggested that Baltimore encourage the U.S. Attorney's Office to move their operation to Baltimore County and let the city take over the Garmatz Building. But the Feds, none too politely, rejected the idea. Cash-strapped Baltimore could not have afforded to buy it anyway.

Besides, building consultants reported a few years back that other than a few flaws (lack of heating and A/C, the possibility of violent confrontations) the Courthouse was in great shape — well-built with sturdy walls and thick, oak doors throughout. So the members of the city government, who usually only visit the courthouse to plead "not guilty" to something everyone knows they did, decided to spend the money designated for the Mitchell's renovation on whatever projects they thought would benefit them the most come the next election.

I can only guess that it was the sturdy walls and thick oak doors that kept anyone from hearing the shot that killed Judge Phillip Hanover of Circuit Court Part 7 late one Monday evening.

No one suspected anything was amiss until nine-thirty the following morning when Judge Hanover failed to ring to let the court bailiff know he was ready to start the day's proceedings. While the judge had his quirks, likes, and dislikes, and could at times be mercurial, he was known for his punctuality. Come nine twenty-nine, he'd hit the buzzer and one minute later he'd emerge from his chambers to the cry of "All rise. Criminal Court Part 7 is now in session. Judge Phillip Hanover presiding." He would then settle himself behind his bench and have his bailiff call the first case. And may God have mercy on any lawyer who was not present or not ready to proceed, for Judge Hanover would not. Some attorneys did not know that bench warrants could be issued for them until the judge did so.

So punctual was the judge that on those rare days when he was a few minutes late those in the know would check their watches or silenced phones and wonder if they were broken.

But on that Tuesday, as the minutes went by – five, ten, fifteen – the bailiff began to worry, both about the judge and the consequences of interrupting him. Finally, at the twenty-minute mark, Bailiff Green knocked on the door of the Judge's chambers and went in. His "Your Honor, is everything all…" was cut short by a loud gasp. Bailiff Green then emerged from the chambers pale and panicky, barely able to tell the sheriff's deputy on duty to "Call Code Black, get police and medics."

Thinking *Not again*, Deputy Bill Perry, in a practiced move, took out and turned on his radio and called the code. Within minutes, the Mitchell Courthouse was locked down, no one to enter or leave, with those inside sheltering in place.

Naturally, a small crowd gathered around the courtroom door

to the judge's chambers. With Bailiff Green standing guard, Deputy Perry first made sure that the judge was beyond medical help then checked the chambers' hallway door. Finding it unlocked, he secured it then relieved Green at guard duty.

That's when Deputy Bill Perry had his moment, his one claim to fame. (Two if you count his being on the scene of another courthouse murder.) When someone in the crowd asked, "What's wrong with the judge, why is he late?" Perry replied,

"Because he is now the Late Judge Phillip Hanover and always will be."

At first, those of us in the SAO's office on Baltimore Street knew something was going on in the Mitchell but weren't quite sure what it was. We'd heard everything from an accidental discharge to a prisoner escape to mass casualties. We did get word that both the Mitchell Courthouse and Courthouse East were closed for the day, said news being the cause of great rejoicing in that it gave the overburdened Assistant State's Attorneys a day to catch up on work that should have been completed the week before.

Soon, though, cell phones started ringing, chirping, screaming, and making all those other noises that people use to let them know a call, text, or tweet was coming in. The news that Judge Hanover had been killed sobered us for a few moments, but then speculation started about who might have killed him. Betting pools were begun which most people denounced as being in bad taste even as they put their money down on the who and the why.

The lockdown lasted for about two hours, just long enough for the BPD and the Sherriff's Office to determine that the judge appeared to be the only person targeted and that there was no active shooter. People not involved were allowed to leave on a floor by floor, room by room basis but only after they were scanned for firearms. No guns were found, but three knives, four multi-tools, two pairs of knitting needles, and a set of throwing stars were confiscated, leaving one to wonder how they were smuggled in.

Officers, detectives, and other people whose positions allowed them to go armed in the courthouse were subject to more intense scrutiny. They had to surrender their weapons for inspection. If it wasn't the same caliber as the one that killed the judge (9mm based on the recovered cartridge case) no problem. If they were carrying a nine, their names and information on their pistols were recorded in case test-fires needed to be performed later.

While this was going on, Homicide detectives were busy on the scene – interviewing the people who were waiting in Part 7 that day, finding out who had worked the night before, and sending uniformed officers to ask courthouse personnel if they had seen anyone who wasn't supposed to be where they were.

The Crime Scene Unit was busy working its magic – taking digital photographs which would be available to all within a few hours of their return to headquarters, swabbing for DNA, processing suitable surfaces for latent prints (in that order), and searching for and collecting anything that might be evidence.

(Back when I was a CSI, I was once asked by a defense attorney how I determined what might be evidence. Since he had not been very polite and had insisted that I come in on my day off for a pre-trail conference, I told him, "Anything loose is considered evidence. Anything that can be pried up is considered loose." Two weeks later, during my testimony I gave a much more professional answer.)

And this being a dead judge rather than just an average citizen shot on the street, CSU did a 360° laser scan of the judge's courtroom, his chambers, and the hallway outside them.

None of this concerned me very much. I had left crime scene work years ago (not entirely voluntarily). I worked as a private investigator for a while until it became clear that I needed a steady income and better working hours. (Falling in love and getting married will do that to the best of us.) So with the help of a Homicide Lieutenant who was willing to overlook my past sins, I became the head of SAO's Forensic Investigation Unit. (And thanks to budget cuts, its sole member.)

So as far as I was concerned that bright and sunny Tuesday, my only involvement in the murder of Judge Phillip Hanover was reading about it in *The Baltimore Truth* and watching it on Action

News.

I should have known better. I was busy reading lab reports from a double homicide that the killer had clumsily tried to disguise as a murder/suicide when my supervisor, Sharon Manchester, called me.

"Matthew, you've been summoned."

"What happened? Did they reopen the Angel Collins case and I'm going to have to tell the truth?"

"No," she said with some exasperation. The Collins case was still a sore point and some people, including Sharon and our boss, Celina Alston, the State's Attorney for Baltimore City, rightly suspected that I knew more about it than I was telling. "You're needed in Part 3. Something about Judge Hanover's murder."

But that was in Part 7, I thought. Part 3 was … damn, it was Judge Devereux's court. How the hell was she involved?

Thirty minutes later I found out.

Judge Gertrude Devereux was a courthouse legend. She started out as one the few black women working for the Public Defender's Office. A few years later she switched sides and joined the SAO. Contrary to one of the myths that grew around her, it was not because she had once been mugged only to be assigned to defend her attacker. First of all, the latter would not have been permitted. As for the former, yes, she was once mugged. She'd lived in Baltimore all her long life. Stop in any courtroom when they're doing juror *voir dire* and watch how many people raise their hands when asked if they've ever been the victim of a crime. It would be easier to ask who hadn't been.

No, Gertrude Devereux became a prosecutor when she realized that the deck was stacked against defendants, particularly the poor, black ones who made up most of her clients. Remember, the presumption of innocence states that a defendant is innocent *until* proven guilty. Not *unless*, but *until*. This presupposes that they will be found guilty.

Now you may not believe that but Gertrude Devereux did and became an ASA to give everyone a fair shake. If she had a reasonable doubt about a defendant's guilt she'd drop the charges.

This did not make her popular with the police or the SAO, but her attitude was enough to get her elected to the Circuit Court, knocking off a sitting judge who thought his job was safe.

Since her election, Judge Devereux applied her principles to the cases she heard. She was, as they say, "tough but fair." She did not suffer fools gladly, or at all. And pity any professional witness who came to court late or unprepared or any lawyer who tried to play the usual games. It is said that the judge held the East Coast record for the number of lawyers fined or jailed for contempt.

It was eerie walking into a mostly empty courthouse. No lawyers, witnesses, or jurors – just bored Deputy Sheriffs who didn't even bother to look at the ID I waved at them. (*This is how weapons get in*, I thought). The marble hallways were so silent that if this were a movie you'd hear the music that told you that something bad was lurking around the next corner.

It wasn't lurking. It was just waiting for me in Judge Devereux's chambers.

I had been in her chambers twice before. The first time was when I was a PI and she held me in contempt for refusing to reveal my client's name to the police and the Grand Jury. This forced me to solve the case from a holding cell using only my memory and a note pad. I did the big reveal in her office, the killer confessed, and to this day no one but me and my client knows who hired me.

The second time the judge was my client. Devereux is a noted collector of true crime memorabilia. She hired me to find a certain umbrella. I found it and delivered it to her chambers. When it came time to settle up I halved my usual fee on the condition that when the time came, and may it not come anytime soon, she'd leave me the umbrella in her will.

When I walked into her chambers for the third time I didn't notice the two men sitting in front of her desk. Instead, I took a moment to look around. A third human skull had joined the two that were there the last time. She had some new wanted posters. The Ed Gein ashtray was still on her desk and there were several canes and one umbrella in the elephant leg stand by the door. One of the canes had belonged to a certain Belgian detective the judge had once met and another was once owned by a man nicknamed Bat. The umbrella was of, course, the one I had found for her. It had the initials "JP" engraved on a band below the handle and had been involved in more than one murder. Sherlock Holmes may have solved the disappearance of James Phillimore, but I had recovered his umbrella.

"Mister Grace, if you are finished looking around we need your talents. Please be seated."

There were three chairs in front of her desk. I took the empty one.

The other two on my side of Devereux's desk were occupied by Deputy Assistant State's Attorney Ogden Manners and Quentin Barnabas, chief legal counsel for the Baltimore Police Department.

Manners was a tall, handsome man who wore his off-the-rack suits as if they were Saville Row Bespoke. His legal credentials were supposed to be top-notch. His chief job as second in command of the SAO was to act as executive toady for Celina Alston. Someone, not me, once said that if you kissed him you'd taste her shoe polish. I wonder if he knows that anytime I wanted to, I could get him indicted for evidence tampering and obstruction of justice.

Barnabas was just the opposite. Short where Manners was tall, dark-skinned instead of light. He also wore off-the-rack suits and if you put a Saville Row Bespoke on him it would look off-the-rack by the end of the day.

Unlike Manners, Barnabas was a great guy with a wonderful sense of humor who embraced the name his Dark Shadows loving parents gave him by dressing up as a vampiric werewolf every Halloween. He also used his mild-mannered appearance to his best advantage, often lulling opposing council into a false sense of superiority.

And then there was me, Matthew Grace, ex-CSI, ex-PI, now mostly a paper pusher with an impressive title, and neither of the two men on my side of the desk looked happy to see me.

"Would one of you gentlemen care to recap or shall I?"

"Your Honor…"

Devereux cut Manners's protest short. "You were poorly

named, Mister Manners, since you don't seem to have any. I have listened to your objections, and yours as well, Mister Barnabas. Blame yourselves for coming to me instead of working things out. Another word from either of you …" She left the unspoken threat dangle for a moment. "I am sure Mister Grace would like to spend some more time looking over my collection and wondering what to bid on when I die while I summon others from your office and have you escorted to a shared holding cell, but I'd rather get this done. Mister Grace …"

"I like the Masterson cane."

"You would. Cole Williams told me what you did to him with the replica you once owned."

"He deserved it."

"I'm sure he did. You are, of course, aware of the murder of Judge Hanover."

"Yes, but not the details."

"Well, his death has created a jurisdictional dispute. Mister Barnabas holds that allowing the SAO to become involved in the investigation would create a conflict of interest, since one or more members of its office may become suspects. And Mister Manners believes that, given the history between the two offices, the BPD may slant their investigation in such a way as to incriminate the SAO to cover up any illegal actions of its officers."

"So, let the State Police handle it. It would give them something to do other than write speeding tickets."

"That's one idea. Mine is to appoint a special investigator, one equally trusted, or mistrusted, by both sides, one answerable only to the court, that is, me." I had the sudden feeling that that bad thing was about to unlurk and bite me in the butt. "Congratulations, Mister Grace, you are now the court-appointed chief investigator of the Phillip Hanover case."

"Your Honor, I don't think …"

"Neither did these two, Mister Grace, and they expressed their thoughts quite vocally until just before your arrival. But consider this, before your 'sudden departure' from the BPD, you were one of the best crime scene people the Laboratory Division had. And you did quite well as a private investigator, even solving a few murders ahead of the police. And I understand that you have assisted the SAO in one or two matters."

I had, neither one of which endeared me to Manners's currently out of town boss.

"Just doing my job, Your Honor."

"A job, Mister Grace, for which you hold the title 'Forensic Investigator.' So, go investigate. As of now you are on a leave of absence from your SAO duties and have been contracted by this court as its investigator. I assume your PI license is still valid?"

"Yes, Your Honor."

"Then you will be paid your old rate adjusted for inflation." I looked over at Masterson's cane. "We'll see, but not until I die. Gentlemen …" The way the judge said this last implied a question mark at the end. "You have one hour to prepare a briefing for Mister Grace, after which he will tell you what he wants your respective departments to do. If there is a lack of cooperation I will hold you two personally responsible. You begin tomorrow, Mister Grace. See me in the morning for all authorizations and warrants. That is all."

After two reluctant "Thank you, Your Honors" I decided to start work immediately.

"Excuse me, Gentlemen." (No question mark.) "I assume that Part 7 is still a closed scene." Neither knew. "Please arrange a 24-hour guard on the courtroom doors and the inner and hallway doors of Judge Hanover's chambers. Two officers each, one Deputy Sheriff and one BPD officer. No one enters for any reason and I want a list of those who try. Thank you. I'll see you in an hour."

After they left without thanking me, Judge Devereux said, "Don't let me or Phillip down, Mister Grace."

"I'll try not to, Your Honor, for your sake and his."

And mine for that matter, I thought. If I screwed this up I'd be working security at my wife's hotel while maybe doing some PI work on the side.

That night I discussed what I knew about the case with my wife Linda, saying "Yes, Dear" to her "Be careful, Matthew." We were settling down to watch the evening news when the phone rang.

"Chief Investigator Grace?" The was some amusement in the voice.

The voice belonged to Joshua Parker, the homicide lieutenant I previously mentioned. I didn't wonder how he heard about my temporary assignment (I hoped it was temporary). By now the word had spread and I'm sure Celina Alston was in her Chicago hotel cursing both my name and Judge Devereux's with equal vehemence.

"Barnabas told you?"

"He didn't have to. I got two calls and one text before he got back to headquarters." He paused, then said the one thing I never expected. "What do you need, Grace? Hanover was a good man, both as an ASA and later as a judge. Whatever it is, just ask."

"The usual in this kind of case, Deacon. Two or three of your best detectives tearing the judge's personal life apart to find who wanted him dead." Before he could respond to that I added. "Of course, if your guys find out who killed him, you get full credit. If not, just send me the reports without sharing with the brass."

"Command is not going to like that, Grace."

"Tell them Judge Devereux has issued a gag order."

"Has she?"

"She will by tomorrow, and it will apply to the SAO as well. One leak anywhere and someone gets Devereux's contempt of court goodie bag."

"Be funny if She got one."

"She" was Celina Alston. Neither Parker nor anyone else in the BPD has referred to her by name since she started trying to put cops in jail.

"Stranger things have happened, Lieutenant."

"Yes, they have. I'll be praying for your success. Don't let me down, Matthew."

"Matthew." Parker hasn't called me by my first name since my wedding. This must be important to him.

I had no sooner hung up when my phone rang again. This time it was Sharon Manchester.

"What the Hell, Matthew?"

"Not my idea, Sharon. Blame Devereux."

"My blaming anyone is not going to help. Manners came back breathing fire. Fire being one of the things he wanted to do to you. Believe it or not, when he called Celina and made that suggestion she told him that would only make it look like the SAO had something to hide."

"The SAO as a lot to hide, Sharon, and one day it will all come out. But not this day, not this time, unless someone there killed the judge. Anything else?"

"Just, be careful, Matthew."

"I always am, Sharon."

"No, you're not." With that, she hung up.

I had had my phone on speaker. Having heard most of the conversation Linda said, "She's right, you're not always careful."

Before I could reply, she crawled close to me on the couch and wrapped her arms around me. "You're supposed to have a nice, safe, boring job where nothing bad happens to you. Now, well, you're back to dealing with gang bosses, investigating murders, and, I think, trying to put your boss in jail."

I couldn't deny the first two, as for the last, maybe I was, if by "my boss" Linda meant Alston and not Sharon. One day it might come to that. For now, I just wanted enough on her to protect myself if she came after me. As for right then,

I hugged Linda tight and said, "I'll be as careful as I can," then I kissed her. The kiss went on longer than either of us thought it would. When we broke it, Linda said, "I've never slept with a chief investigator before."

"Well, you won't be able to say that tomorrow morning." We kissed again, and that's all you need to know about what happened that evening.

The next morning I called Cole Williams, the man who, once upon a time when we were both kids, I hit with a replica Bat Masterton cane. Like me, he now works as an investigator for the State's Attorney's office, only he has a badge and carries a gun. I dislike guns and in my job I don't need a badge.

"Cole," I said. "How would you like to do some real work instead of reading police reports and chasing down witnesses."

"Let me guess. You want me and maybe one or two others to question courthouse employees about what they may know about Judge Hanover's murder, and pick up as much gossip and rumors about the man as possible."

"You got it, Cole."

"Will it piss off Alston?"

"Alston, Manners, a few others."

"Then I'm in, and I'll probably have a waiting list for people willing to help. What about the other judges?"

Good question. Judges are and always will be special cases. Despite being elected officials, they can mostly do what they like with very little oversight. It's only when one of them greatly exceeds the bounds of propriety that anyone outside the world of the courthouse takes notice. Unlike other politicians, the media mostly ignores them. Come election times, they are the only office seekers whose records are not discussed. Most voters don't even realize judges are elected until it's time to fill out their ballots, and then they either ignore them or blindly vote the full slate.

"Seems to me that talking to judges is the job of the Chief Investigator," Cole offered. I had to agree with him. With great power, etc. I decided to start with Judge Devereux when I saw her later that morning and ask her to pave the way with her colleagues. To Cole I said,

"I take the judges. You guys start with their clerks, see what they know, or at least what they'll willing to tell you."

"Will do. When do you want all this?"

"Yesterday. It's that kind of case."

"And it's all yours." Then he laughed as if we were finally even for that whack in the head I gave him so many years ago.

After my talk with Cole but before my walk over to Part 3, I thought of a way to make my life easier. I thought of two ways, actually, but I wasn't ready for a career in hotel security. And I'd given my word to Gertrude Devereaux.

So plan A. I created a document and emailed it to Devereaux.

I was getting ready to go see her when Sharon poked her head into my closet of an office.

"Matthew, I don't know how to tell you this .."

"Then don't. The less I know the less I'll have to testify to."

She didn't smile. "It's Ogden. This morning he told me to tell you that since you are on a leave of absence you need to vacate your office." Sharon paused before giving me the rest of the bad news. "And since you're not on the payroll he's canceling your health insurance and other benefits."

I had expected something like that and was, of course, ready. "Was this his idea or Alston's? Never mind. Please inform Manners that last night I logged into my Baltimore City employee account and put in for five leave days. So that keeps me on the payroll and if he or anyone else cancels my benefits they can take it up with the Labor Commissioner. She's a very nice lady. I once did some divorce work for her. The dirt I found on her now ex-husband got her a very nice settlement. As for this office, let me just get some personal items and I'll be gone. Of course, I'll have to explain all this to Judge Devereaux when I ask her for office space."

I packed up the laptop I had brought from home and some incriminating evidence against well, among others, the man who just kicked me out of my office. I then locked down my computer and walked up Calvert Street to the Mitchell Courthouse.

Judge Devereaux was in her office waiting for me. "Let's make this fast, Mister Grace. I have a courtroom full of people awaiting justice."

She then gave me a handful of documents – my official appointment as a court investigator, warrants for Judge Hanover's home, vehicles, chambers, and "all electronic devices contained therein."

"Justice will have to wait, Your Honor. I have some questions to ask as well as a favor."

No, the favor wasn't about office space. I decided to let that one go. Manners was a pain but in this case I think he might have been right. Not I would tell him that. Let him sweat a contempt charge.

"Ask away, Mister Grace."

"First of all, I emailed you a questionnaire I would like you to forward to your fellow judges. Rather than wait for them to agree to see me so I can ask impertinent questions the questionnaire covers that. Their whereabouts when Judge Hanover was killed. Their professional relationship with the judge. Their personal relationship, if any. Are they aware of anyone who had had a violent or suspicious argument with the judge? Are they aware of any less than professional behavior by the judge that may have led to his death? And, of course, where were they when Judge Hanover was killed?"

"And when was that?"

"According to the preliminary report from the Medical Examiner, around six the previous evening."

Pulling up the email, Devereaux looked it over. "Yes, I see it here. You're asking them to account for their time between 4:30 that evening until just before Phillip's body was found. Well, this seems reasonable, efficient, and shows some consideration. I'm sure, on my recommendation, my colleagues will cooperate. But what if they don't?"

"Then I'll ask Lieutenant Joshua Parker to assign some investigators to rip their lives apart. They can also expect an article in *The Baltimore Truth* about how certain judges are refusing to cooperate in the murder of one of their own."

The judge smiled. "Then I will strongly advise them to cooperate. And if they do, what then?"

"I review their statements, compare them to other information I've obtained, and check alibis. If I catch them in a lie I promote them from judge to suspect."

"Very nice, Mister Grace. May I go now?"

I shook my head. "As long as I'm here, Your Honor, what was your personal relationship with Judge Hanover/"

"What makes you think I had one?"

"Yesterday you called him 'Phillip.' If he wasn't a friend of yours, you would have called him 'Judge Hanover'."

It was a chance shot but it struck home. Judge Devereaux nodded and sat back in her chair. "I met Phillip in law school.

We've been friends, close friends, ever since."

"How close? Were there benefits involved?"

If the judge took offense at my asking her if she'd ever had sex with the murder victim she didn't show it. Of course, I may have blown my shot at the Bat Masterson cane.

"Just friends, Mister Grace. Phillip was not one for long-term relationships. Neither was I at the time we met. Not until I met the man who would become my first husband." She then sighed. "Unfortunately, as it turned out neither my first nor my second marriage could be considered 'long-term.' One would think I would have been a better judge of men."

I smiled at this as the judge went on. "And to anticipate your next question, on the day Phillip was killed, I was in court, jury *voir dire*, until 6:00. Then a sheriff's deputy walked me out to St. Paul Street and stayed with me until my Uber picked me up. The driver will tell you that he got me home at 7:00. And now, Mister Grace, I must really start court. I'll send out your survey at the lunch break. You'll have your replies by tomorrow, the next day at the latest."

I was dismissed, but still needed an office. I called Parker who told me that CSU was finished with Hanover's chambers.

"We got all we could out of it, Grace. As you're the chief investigator I thought I'd leave its ransacking to you. Let me know if you find a death threat or suicide note."

So I had an office. I was going to spending a lot of time there anyway so why not?

The guards I had ordered were still on duty. According to their logs, other than CSU and detectives no one had tried to get in. I showed them my ID and entered.

The judge's chambers looked like every other inside crime scene after the techs had done their work. Fingerprint powder covered every flat, reasonably non-porous surface. Rectangles in the powder showed where lifts had been made – the file cabinets, the inside knob of the door leading to the hallway, the glass covering the top of the judge's desk. The carpet looked like it had been vacuumed for trace evidence, and surfaces that would likely have been touched had no doubt been swabbed for DNA. I wondered if the crime scene people had checked the computer keyboard for trace evidence. I got some printer paper, upended the keyboard over it, and shook it like an Etch-a-Sketch. Nothing fell out so I supposed they had.

I spent the next half hour going over the crime scene unit's work. I even checked the windows. They were locked tight. Opening one up and looking out, I could see that there was no easy climb up and that it was too high to safely jump out of.

CSU hadn't missed a thing. Not that I had expected them to, but it never pays to double-check. All in all, it was a very thorough job, more than most crime scenes got. Of course, most crime scenes didn't have a dead judge on the carpet.

Hanover's papers were next. Actually, cleaning my work surfaces was next. The crime lab spreads powder, it does not clean it up. Knowing this, I had brought the right kind of spray cleaner and paper towels, a lot of paper towels. An hour later I was ready to ransack.

No death threats, no documents incriminating anyone known or unknown. Except for two file drawers, no personal papers at all. One drawer had information about his time on the bench. Nineteen years ago he had been appointed to serve out the term of Judge Isaac Norris, who had died in his robes just after gaveling court into session. Three years later, Hanover was elected to his own fifteen-year term, and last year had won reelection. The drawer mostly contained campaign literature, fund-raising information, lists of donors and their contributions, that sort of thing. The donor list could have served as a roster of the lawyers who practiced their craft in Baltimore City. More than half the names on the list were not familiar to me – assistant state's attorneys, public defenders, and private attorneys. Some had kicked in the maximum amount allowed, others contributed just enough to get their names on the list. I'm sure the other circuit court judges had similar lists. The ones who had run with Hanover would have an identical list as sitting judges tend to run as a bloc. Not that contributions to their campaign funds would sway a judge's decision one way or the other but why take chances?

Hanover's other drawer was half-filled with documents relating to health insurance, retirement benefits, and the like. The other half contained the judge's cookie stash – chocolate chip and oatmeal raisin. The judge didn't need them anymore and since there was no sense in letting them go to waste, I had a snack before going back to work.

I think it's a law that bookcases filled with law books and legal journals must cover one wall in every lawyer's office and every judge's chambers, even though everything contained in said journals and books is available online. I looked at the shelves of voluminous tomes and considered if I should go through each and every one in search of a hidden document or photograph. That's where the clues usually are in mystery novels and on TV. But with them, there's always one volume out of place and only the main character notices. As the court-appointed main character, I felt it my duty to at least look at the books. Nothing out of place, everything in numerical or alphabetical order. I decided that looking through each book page by page would be my final act of desperation just before I told Judge Deveraux that I was out of ideas and had let her and "Phillip" down.

Then I checked out Hanover's computers. There was a city-owned desktop and what was probably the judge's laptop. I turned them on and waited. I expected both to ask for passwords. I had even brought a USB drive loaded with hacking software just in case. But both computers opened right up. I guess the judge thought that locking his chambers' doors was enough security.

I spent the next hour going through the desktop and found it was nothing more than a digital version of the judge's file cabinets – work-related emails; invitations to dinners, speaking engagements, and conferences; copies of letters back and forth between him and his colleagues; and digital versions of his decisions along with the results of any appeals. His browser history showed only court-related webpages, including links to most if not all the books on his shelves.

Unlike the judge's filing cabinet, his desktop did not contain anything about his judicial campaigns. That would probably be on his laptop, since you're not supposed to use city resources when you're running for office.

I broke for lunch, trusting the very vulnerable laptop to the guards protecting Hanover's chambers. When I got back, it was right where I left it, the hair I left on the mouse undisturbed.

With some exceptions, there was nothing on Hanover's laptop you wouldn't find on yours. He had a respectable win percentage in a few solitaire games but wasn't that good at Mahjong. There were PowerPoint links on his desktop for when he gave talks. There was nothing remarkable in his Word or Excel folders.

His email was nothing special, although he needed a stronger spam filter. His "old mail" and "sent" files went back a few years and in them I found semi-passionate exchanges between the judge and a variety of women, none of the women overlapping and none of the exchanges lasting longer than a few months. One was still ongoing but approaching the record of six months. On reading the last few emails of each affair, none of them ended with bitter recriminations or anything close to a death threat.

None of the judge's correspondents used emails that revealed their names. No firstname.lastname@judgelovers.com or anything like that. Probably special emails just for the duration of the affairs. I thought about emailing the women myself but didn't want to tip things. So I made notes of the addresses and planned to ask Sharon to write up subpoenae for the various email providers so I could put names with addresses. If that didn't work I'd have one of my pirate friends get the information "unofficially." Then I'd turn them over to Parker's detectives as part of my request to "tear the judge's personal life apart."

Hanover had an Amazon account and his tastes ran to jazz and science fiction and fantasy. He subscribed to Netflix and Amazon Prime Video and his viewing tastes ran to light comedies and old cartoons. His social media was remarkably apolitical.

But I had mentioned exceptions. In his saved favorites were several sites that featured nude women. Some were professional sites but most were of the amateur variety. No porn and no underaged girls. His browser history showed that he visited each site almost every day and downloaded heavily from each of them.

Downloaded to where? The folder wasn't hard to find. Why should he hide it? No one but him had access to his computer. There was a shortcut on his screen named "Special A" that led me right to it. And yes, there was another shortcut named "Special B." The latter led to a multi-paged spreadsheet with numbers and dates and amounts in black and red. He was tracking something – stocks, gambling (I know, much the same thing), something to do with his taxes or salary? Or maybe he was the obsessive type who kept track of fines given out vs. fines paid. I decided to look at that later. But first, the naked ladies.

I know what you're thinking, why is he wasting time looking at naked women when there's a murder to solve? I wondered that myself but then realized that this was the first chink in Hanover's armor I'd found and maybe I could use it to find the man inside. I opened the file.

There were a lot of naked women in that folder, so many that Hanover had subfolders for each year. I opened one at random and viewed the details. Apparently, he'd been checking out the adult sites and downloading as a way to start his day and during lunch. I switched to the extra-large icons view and scanned the pics.

The judge's tastes ran mostly to young slender, white women but other races, sizes, and ages were well-represented. No sexual activity of any kind was depicted and the few men who appeared in the pics were shown just standing next to the women.

I checked out a few more years and found more of the same. Different women, different locations, vintage nudes mixed in with modern ones. All anonymous and none having anything to do with the case.

As I scrolled to the bottom I noticed two subfolders weren't dated. One was named "Stars" and the other "Personal."

"Stars" was exactly that – celebrity nudes from movies, TV, magazines, and phone hacks. Resisting the urge to check out some of my favorite actresses, I closed that one and opened "Personal."

Not as many women but more pics of each. Some were vacation shots – on the beach, at a resort, posing with costumed characters at theme parks and cosplayers in Times Square. Others were, as the folder's name stated, more personal – photos taken in hotel rooms or secluded areas, the women in and out of sexy lingerie. There were also pictures of most of the women that were all taken in the same bedroom or bathroom. Some were posed and others seemed to be candids with the subject unaware that she was being photographed. Some of the women in the candids did not appear nude in any posed shots taken in hotels or out of doors.

Suddenly I felt like a teenaged boy who had just peeped his first window and was now suffering from good, old-fashioned Catholic guilt. I did not want to go on. The women in these photos did not know they were being photographed or thought the pictures would be seen only by their lover. I did not want to further invade their privacy but one of them might have found out the judge already had and was looking at them on a regular basis. The ones who posed for the pics may not have cared, they may even have some of the judge, but if one of the women who were only in the candids found out, that knowledge may have been enough to cause her to pull the trigger.

I went to my laptop and opened the photos that CSU had taken in the judge's house during the search made by Parker's team. The same bedroom, the same bathroom. I called Parker.

"Deacon, would you please send cyber forensics back to the judge's house." I told him what they had to look for. "Send someone you trust, better still, go yourself if you can. I need the cameras and the device they were being sent to. And I'll need his cell phone as well. Where is that?"

"In Evidence Control, waiting for you to ask for it."

"Thanks. And tell the CF teams that if anything they find gets out, angels will weep for them."

"What are you hoping to find, Grace?"

"At the worst, dirty pictures. At best, a threat of bodily harm."

Which would probably not be admissible in court, since a judge, an officer of the court, recorded the subject without her knowledge. But that would be a problem for the lawyers.

Forcing myself to get back to the pictures, I took another look at them. They were identified by two or three initials followed by a number – PTF01, PTFO2, etc. Presumably, the judge knew who they were. As I looked at them I realized that so did I, two of them at least.

The first, a file labeled "GS." Gloria Swoboda. Everyone called her "Glory." She and my supervisor Sharon had dated for a time. Glory was a good-looking brunette who, like Sharon, worked as an ASA. That's how the two met. Maybe that's how she and the judge met as well.

Sharon and Glory didn't stay together long. "She was fun, Matthew," Sharon said when she told me about their break-up, "but I wasn't into some of the things she wanted me to try." Sharon didn't volunteer what those things were and I didn't ask.

The one good thing Sharon got out of their relationship was Sophie Doyle. Sophie was a paramedic for the Baltimore City Fire Department who testified in one of Glory's cases. Glory introduced her to Sharon and now the two are engaged.

The pics of Glory were, well, explicit, that's all I'm going to say about them other then she knew she was posing for them. That alone might eliminate her as a suspect but I debated about calling Sharon, swearing her to secrecy, and telling her about the pics of Glory.

The second. A file labeled GD. Scanned from old Polaroid instant photos. Before the digital age, Polaroids were how lovers took naughty pics of each other when they didn't want to embarrass the film developer. These were not as explicit as Glory's. In fact, they were somewhat demure. If one could call full nudes of a young, black, law student demure. Maybe artistic was the word.

I looked at the computer clock. It was getting close to five, almost quitting my time. Still, I looked over the "Personal" pics to see if I might recognize anyone else. No luck. But I hadn't had close contact with most of the ASA's since my Crime Lab days. Maybe when the subpoenae came though I'd be able to put names with the, er, faces.

Then I saw it. Maybe it had been willful blindness, maybe I just couldn't believe it. A third folder. CA. Celina Alston. Only these pics weren't taken in the judge's bedroom. These were taken in the judge's chambers, some in the same chair where I was sitting.

Damn. Now I'd have to talk to Sharon. But first I had to set up a meeting with Judge Gertrude Devereaux who, going by some Polaroid photos, was quite the looker in her day. I wonder why she lied to me.

"Because I was ashamed, Mister Grace," an embarrassed Judge Devereaux explained the next morning.

After seeing the photos of her I felt that we at least should be Matt and Gertie, but I refrain from suggesting this. However I did remark, "I don't know why. From what I saw you had nothing to be ashamed about."

The judge looked at me as if ready to cite me for contempt. Instead, she just smiled ruefully and said, "I was a looker but my beauty faded."

I shook my head. "Looks fade, beauty does not. And except for lying to your special investigator, you have a beautiful," I took another look around her office, "if somewhat twisted soul, Your Honor. So how long was the affair and why did it end, or did it?"

"A few months, the summer between our second and third years of law school. We decided that we made better friends than lovers and parted amicably. Besides, he wasn't that good in bed. But then again, as young as I was, I probably wasn't either. Fortunately, like fine wine, I improved with age." As I let that one go she added, "Damn him. He told me he had destroyed those photos. What's … going to happen to Phillip's computer?"

She didn't care about the laptop, just certain photos on it. I shrugged. "That depends on how the case plays out. The photos might be evidence, they might not."

She wanted to ask me to delete the photos. She didn't. I liked her, as a judge and as a person and so I wanted to delete them. I couldn't.

"Am I a suspect?"

Of course, she was. I had paced out her alibi before I knocked on the door of her chambers. Ten minutes from her door to Hanover's.

With nobody in the hallway, a quick knock, he opens the door, she shoots and scores, then back to her chambers to be escorted to St. Paul Street.

In answer to her question, I handed her a document I'd prepared before coming to her chambers. "Your Honor," I said formally, "I would like you to consent to having your chambers and your home searched for a 9mm pistol and ammunition. Detective Lieutenant Joshua Parker, whom I trust more than I do myself, is standing by and will search your office while you're on the bench. After today's session, he will escort you to your home and search that."

There was that contempt look again followed by another rueful smile. "Quite right and proper, Mister Grace." She took the papers and signed them. "I could have thrown the gun away, you know."

"You throw away a gun that was used to kill a judge?" I took another look around her office. "You'd rather go to jail."

The Deacon's eyes went wide when I asked him to search Devereaux's home and office. I did not tell him why and he did not ask. When he entered her chambers, all Devereaux said to him was, "Please be neat, Lieutenant, and don't forget to leave me a list of what you take."

Devereaux then went to court and Parker went to work. I went back to Judge Hanover's office and on to my next set of problems.

Sharon Manchester did not react to seeing her ex-girlfriend's photos among those collected by Judge Hanover. "It's something she would do. And he's someone she would do. That's one of the reasons we broke up. She wanted to do threesomes, mixed or otherwise. I think two's company and three is one too many."

Then I showed her Alston sitting in the judge's chair.

Sharon does not usually swear, but she made an exception in this case. I think she may even have set the courthouse record for the most vulgarities uttered in a single sentence since Dante Jones was sentenced to multiple life in Part 12 by Judge Anita Esslemont. Okay, maybe they were tied but Sharon was ahead by virtue of originality and lack of repetition.

"So what are you going to do, Matthew?"

That was a good question. So far I had two members of the SAO involved with the judge. That alone called the integrity of any trials over which he presided into question. How many more were there?

Dodging Sharon's question, I asked her to look over the rest of the "Personal" folder, hoping she'd pay little attention to some old Polaroids, especially since Parker's searches had not turned up any 9mm pistols or cartridges. Of course, that didn't clear Deveraux, just made her less likely than Ogden Manners, who could have taken Hanover out to protect Celina Alston's reputation.

Sharon looked over the photos and recognized some.

"MN, that's Maria Newman, an ASA who handles fraud cases. LD is Lois Delgado, she's a public defender. That helps balance the scales, at least. Oh shit, SL is Simone Lee. She was a law clerk. That's not good. None of these are, really, but a judge boffing a law clerk is less good than the others. This one here, CC … let me just…"

Up until then, Sharon had been looking at the thumbnail photos on the folder covers. She doubled clicked the CC folder and brought up all the pics.

"Damn, I thought so but wasn't sure. CC is Judge Cordelia Copper, the queen of Part 19. And this one …" she double-clicked on the AE folder, "… is Judge Esslemont of Part 12."

Sharon put both open folders up at once. "Boy, those robes do hide a lot, don't they?"

Sharon seemed to be having more fun looking at the pics than she should. I can't say that I blamed her, Judge Hanover had an eye for beauty. I ruined her fun by pointing out,

"Isn't Judge Copper married to a state senator?"

"Yeah, that's going to cause problems, isn't it?"

"It might," I agreed. Then I saw something in Judge Esslemont's folder. Like the ones of Celina Alston, the last few pics of her were taken in the Judge's chambers. Switching the view to "Details" I saw that they had been taken recently. There was something about them. They weren't candid shots but they didn't look like the other posed ones.

"Selfie stick," Sharon explained.

Sharon looked over the other objects of Hanover's desires but they were unknown to her.

"We'll know who they are once you send out these subpoenae." I handed her the list of email addresses I needed names for.

She took them saying, "Most people say subpoenas."

"Most people did not have a hard-assed high school Latin teacher."

Sharon looked at the judge's laptop. "This is a mess."

"That it is, Sharon. Right now we have conflict of interest, compromised cases, invasion of privacy, illegal photography, and some serious abuses of power and position. It's no wonder Alston wanted this investigated by the SAO."

"What's going to happen when all this comes out, Matthew?"

"Who says it's going to come out?"

She gave me that "What do you mean?" look.

I explained. "If I solve this, Alston will press for a guilty plea, if only to keep the photos of her from coming out. If she gets it and an in-chambers allocution, the laptop goes into Evidence Control where it will probably lie forgotten. Is that right? No. but it's the way our State's Attorney does business. And speaking of Alston, is she still in Chicago?" Sharon nodded. "Call her, tell her what was found. Suggest it would not hurt if she consented to a quiet search of her home and office for form's sake. A search warrant can too easily go public."

"She might agree to that. But what if she doesn't?"

"A search warrant can too easily go public," I repeated pointedly. "But tell her that right now she's not a suspect." (Manners was, but no need to mention that.) "Just another box to check."

"But what about …?" she pointed to the CA folder.

"Misconduct, but consensual. It's these three I worry about."

I pointed to the folders of Delgado, Newman, and Copper. "These three didn't know they were starring on Candid Camera."

"Search warrants?"

"A private word first. They didn't agree to be photographed. Maybe they'll agree to be searched."

After Sharon left for her Baltimore Street office to make what had to be the phone call of a lifetime, Lieutenant Parker called. The cyber techs had found three micro-cameras, two in the judge's bedroom and one in the bathroom. "And per your instructions, Grace, they'll be sent to you untouched, along with a portable hard drive and the judge's cell, which the cell phone forensic techs were just about work on."

"Thank you, Lieutenant. Thanks too for searching Deveraux's office and home."

"Anything for her, Grace. She's one of the good guys, even if what's in her home is stranger than what's in her chambers."

"I hope you took pictures."

"I had my body cam running the whole time."

I then made Parker's day by telling him about the other searches he might have to do.

"Her? Really." Then it hit him. I should have known he was too good a detective not to add up micro-cameras, cell phones, and search warrants to the right answer. "Her and the judge. Damn." Parker was a deacon in his church. He didn't lie or swear. So his "damn" was of higher significance than Sharon's profanity-laced outburst. "When?"

"Not yet, maybe not ever. The bad angel on my left shoulder is still arguing with the good one on my right as to whether it's necessary or just a way of messing with her. The bad angel, well, she's winning but it's going to be close."

"Your angels are female?"

"Aren't they all? Anyway, I'll call you if and when."

"Wait a minute, Grace. Does this mean Deveraux and Hanover …?"

"Goodbye, Deacon."

After I hung up on Parker I closed the laptop and thought about the case. The reports he had sent over had shown no known threats against the judge. No violent felons he had sentenced recently out of prison. His finances were nothing fancy but solid, with no questionable deals or offshore accounts.

That left the naughty pictures as the motive. At least I had a few suspects: Judge Copper, PD Delgado, ASA Newman, and Manners, the latter either working on his own or for Alston.

Opening the judge's laptop I pulled up the photos in "Details" view and compared them against the time frames of the emails. That let me at least match up initials with addresses. Except for Judge Deveraux, Judge Copper was one of the first of his lovers he had photos of. (I made a note to check when she'd gotten married. If was after their affair that was one less issue to worry about.) Judge Esslemont was his most recent love. Theirs was no doubt the still ongoing email exchange. Delgado's and Newman's affairs with the judge were two and three years past.

I decided to add Simone Lee to the list. She had joined the Virginia Commonwealth's Attorney's Office as a prosecutor. Maybe with the Me Too Movement calling nasty SOBs to well-deserved accounts, Ms. Lee decided to confront Judge Hanover about his using his position to take advantage of her. Probably not, she had public opinion and the law on her side if she wanted to make his life hell, but I couldn't discount a heated argument followed by a gunshot. I made a note to check on her whereabouts. I knew some people in Virginia who could do a "routine but discrete" check.

Still, something was bothering me. If it was the pictures, how did the killer find out about them? The judge would not have told them they had been secretly photographed. How likely was it, I wondered, that two of his ex-lovers had somehow compared notes? One day did Judge Esslemont ask Copper how "Phillip" was in bed and had he taken any pics of her?

No, I thought, *something still is not adding up.*

Then it hit me – adding up – and I felt so, so stupid. Judge Hanover had shortcuts to two special folders. One was a boring spreadsheet and the other was filled with naked ladies. And man that I am, I let myself get distracted and did not even consider that by its place on the desktop display, to Judge Hanover, Special B was every bit as important as Special A. Why else would it be special?

I opened the spreadsheet. Page 0 had sequential numbers down the left side. The unnamed headers were obviously debits, credits, and totals going by the entered numbers. Most of the totals almost zeroed out. A few were heavy in the black. None were in the red.

The other pages were numbered, again sequentially starting at one and ending at 34. but some numbers were missing. A comparison with page 0 showed that the same numbers were missing on its left side. The number three wasn't there, neither was seven, a few others were missing as well.

So what part did these sheets play in Judge Hanover's murder, I wondered. What part? Hanover presided over Part 7, Deveraux over Part 3. Both were missing.

I pulled up the Baltimore Bar Association website, checked on the other judges. The judges who missing were all recent appointments.

The "parts" for which there were pages all showed initials down the left side and dates in the headers. The most recent dates were from last year, the year Judge Hanover won reelection. In fact, all of the pages for all of the parts showed dates that were either in an election year or in a year prior to one. I was willing to bet that the initials down the left side of each page represented donors. (I didn't think they were the naked ladies in the other folder.) I went to the file cabinet drawer where the judge kept his campaign material and verified this, at least for the elections in which the judge had run.

It is illegal to use campaign contributions for personal gain. If there's money left over, you can use it in a subsequent election or donate it but you can't buy yourself a new car or house. But as I've already mentioned, judges can mostly do what they like with very little oversight.

It appears that Judge Hanover had come to suspect that some of his colleagues in black were too far in the black when it came to their campaign funds. Based on the date that the Special B folder was created he found out a few months ago. How he found out was yet to be determined.

I've always thought it odd that some people could be morally despicable in some things (spying on one's lovers, sexually harassing subordinates) yet behave properly in others (not misusing campaign funds). Then again, maybe the judge was going to use what he found for his own purposes rather than call in someone like ASA Newman from the SAO Fraud Unit. But whatever his motives, someone may have found out what he was doing and killed him because of it.

But then I ran into the same wall as with the candid nudes. How did that someone find out? I thought about and finally realized that the answer had more or less stared me in the face. I then called Lieutenant Parker and broke his heart by putting the search of Alston's home and office on hold.

The next day the three officers and three deputy sheriffs guarding Judge Hanover's courtroom and chambers were pulled due to "personnel shortages." The locking of the doors was deemed sufficient security.

The room was quiet. Thanks to its thick walls there was no sound from the hallway and the traffic outside could barely be heard. The laptop on the desk was open and ready. I was waiting and watching, thinking back to what wasn't on the judge's phone and what was on the portable hard drive that was delivered yesterday along with the phone and micro-cameras.

Outside Judge Hanover's chambers, the Mitchell Courthouse was shutting down. People were ending their day and going home, which is where I should have been. Playing games with a killer is not in my job description. I had done it once as a crime scene tech and a few times as a PI. The first few times I survived mostly by luck. Fortunately, I tend to learn from my mistakes.

The sound of a key in a lock was quite loud in the quiet room. I sat back in my chair, out of the line of sight of the hallway door.

I watched as the person who entered walked over to the desk and picked up the laptop (not the judge's, something else learned from a past mistake).

"Good evening, Anita."

Judge Esslemont turned, reached into her purse. I showed her the .38 revolver I held in my hand. (I said I disliked guns, not that I didn't have one.)

She dropped her purse, which made a "thud" even on the thick carpet. "That's Judge Esslemont to you, or Your Honor."

"I'll go with Judge Esslemont, since you lost whatever honor you had when you killed Phillip Hanover."

"How dare you?"

"Knock it off, Judge. Your boyfriend's research shows a lot more campaign contributions coming in than going out. And most of that is not in your reserve fund for the next election."

"You have no proof."

I did actually. Hanover had his micro-cameras running for all his intimate bedroom sessions. They downloaded to that portable hard drive. Esslemont was surprised when I quoted her saying, "Don't worry about the money, Philly. What do you think campaign funds are for?"

"That got him thinking, didn't it? But just as you didn't know about the cameras in his bedroom, you didn't know that he was looking into judicial campaign finances. Not until you posed for those selfies when he was out of the office. They were very nice, by the way, especially the ones on his desk next to his laptop. Did he leave the file open or were you snooping around and found it?"

"So what? I was not aware that I was being recorded. So my statement is out. And as for the photos, given who else is on them, do you think they'll ever be shown in court?"

I shrugged. "Don't care, Judge. I've got you breaking into the murder scene with a spare key you're not supposed to have. And from that thud your purse made I'm betting you've got the murder weapon in there."

She bent down as if to grab her purse and the gun inside. "Don't," I warned, showing her my revolver. "We don't need another dead judge sprawled on the carpet."

She straightened up, sighed in resignation. "So read me my rights and I'll call my attorney."

"I think you know your rights." She nodded that she did. "But let's not be hasty. Maybe we can work something out."

All those years on the bench. All those TV shows and movies. Still, she bit. Most of them do when offered "the out."

"Like what?"

"Like half of what's left of your campaign funds. That's for me.

As for my boss, let's just say Celina could use a few wins."

"She's involved in this?"

"Let's just say she doesn't want what's on that computer becoming public any more than you do. Just tell me why you did it and that nine will be found on some recently released loser Judge Hanover sentenced years ago. Just tell me one thing. Why did you kill him? Like the man said to Dirty Harry, I gots to know."

She relaxed. She was safe. I was as crooked as she was. "He was breaking it off. Said six months was a long time. He had a spare key. I took it. I thought the selfies would help. Then I saw the file. He'd left it open. He was always careless about things like that. Didn't even have his computer set to time out to sleep mode. That night, his last night, on my way out I saw that his door was open. I confronted him. He said he was going to send me to jail. I carry the gun for protection. So I sent him to Hell. Anything else, Mister Grace?"

"Just one thing." I didn't have to say it. Judge Esslemont had already admitted to knowing her rights, admitted it right to the micro-cameras I had set up in Hanover's chambers. The micro-cameras that were sending a live feed to the portable hard drive in Judge Deveraux's chambers. I took out the little card I never thought I'd get a chance to use and read it.

"You have the right to remain silent …"

It all played out just as I had told Sharon it would. A guilty plea to manslaughter with five years in medium-security kept the laptop and its contents out of the courtroom and the public eye. The media, especially *The Baltimore Truth*, ate up the whole "courtroom crime of passion" storyline and never questioned the light sentence. As for the laptop, it's in Evidence Control, waiting for the truth to come out. As for Celina Alston, we all pretend that nobody knows about how intimate she was with Judge Hanover's chair, and desk, and carpet. There was just one other thing.

It was only me and Gertrude Deveraux in her chambers. Court was over for the night and we had business.

"Very good, Mister Grace, although since you've seen me in

birthday suit maybe I should call you Matthew."

"And I can call you …"

"Your Honor will do fine. Or Judge. Or if you ever need a favor."

"Thank you, Your Honor. Now may I get back to my real job?"

"You may, but I don't think you'll be happy there for much longer. You're not a paper-pushing kind of man. You'll be getting a check for your work in the mail and here's a bonus."

She handed me a Bat Masterson cane along with a certificate of authenticity. "There's no record of the real Masterson ever using a cane. This one, like the one in my elephant's leg, was a prop on the TV show. Thank you again, Matthew."

"You're welcome, Your Honor."

"And there's one more thing. When I die, in addition to the umbrella, I've decided to leave you my skull."

I looked over to the three on her bookshelf. "Which one?" I asked.

She pointed to her head and said, "This one." I then decided it was time to leave and go back to my boring, paper-pushing job.

JUROR NULLIFICATION

Judge Phillip Hanover's murder was not the first to have occurred in the courthouse. I had only been working for the State's Attorney's Office as a forensic investigator for about six months when the first one happened. I was at Zeke's Coffee Shop on Harford Road with Detective Don Morris …

"It was damn near a dunker, Grace. All we needed was a video of Redman standing over the victim pumping the bullets into him. I mean, we found cigarettes butts with his DNA in the victim's back yard. A street camera had him running away from the scene just minutes after neighbors heard the shots. And five minutes later, when he stops running, he texts to some no-name cell, <It's done and so is he>."

I shook my head. Back when I worked crime scenes for the Baltimore Police we had smarter bad guys, much harder to catch. But then again we didn't have forensic DNA or people with cell phones who had to document their every move.

"Fingerprints?" I asked. I knew the answer but it was his story so he got to tell it.

"Not on the scene, or on the revolver we found a half-mile from Redman's house. But get this, the damned fool wiped the gun but not the cartridges in the chamber. Latents matched the prints found on two of them to Redman. And Firearms matched the gun to the bullets from the body. Damn, Grace, it was as close to perfect as I ever came."

"And Redman didn't go for it?"

Don took a bite of his cinnamon roll and shook his head "Are you kidding? That was the one flaw in the case, at least back then. With what he texted we figured it for a hit. Plus we found two Visa gift cards in his bedroom, both for three grand and bought just before the murder. But even when offered a sweetheart deal he refused to give up any names. His only statements, other than references to my relationships with my mother, and my sister, and my brother, were 'Got nutting to say' and 'Lawyer.' And from what I heard later, he didn't say much more to his public defender, although I don't think the PD's family members got mentioned."

"Drugs?" I asked, just to keep up my side of the conversation.

"What do you think? Redman runs with the Dundalk Dawgs but they have a lot of members. Down there it's a city/county, black/white thing and they're hard to keep track of. When questioned, the ones we did find replied in much the same manner as Redman. 'Nuttin' and 'Lawyer'."

"But you still had a dunker."

"Yeah, I did. And I had Judge Gertrude Devereux presiding in Part 3 over the case of State vs. Boles Redman."

Judge Devereux's presence meant that the trial should have been straight forward, no grandstanding, no frivolous objections, no pointless questioning – in short, nothing that would hamper the fair and swift, emphasis on the swift, administration of justice. Juries loved Judge Devereux; cops and witnesses did as well, unless the former came unprepared and the latter were obviously lying. Don didn't lie – well, not on or for the job – not working for Lieutenant Joshua Parker. Any of Parker's detectives who strayed too far from the truth wound up reassigned to the district furthest from their home.

"So the trial promised to be fast and easy," Don told me. "No witnesses to lie, not show up, or get confused by the defense attorney. Other than the responding officers to set the scene, no police on the stand for the jurors not to trust. Just cold, hard facts presented by civilian forensic experts supported by science and technology. You know how it is. Thanks to all the TV shows on the subject, jurors love science and technology and expect to see it in court. Sometimes the CSI effect works for us instead of against us."

"So what went wrong?"

Don took another bite of his roll, had another sip of Zeke's Charm City Blend. "We were expecting a four-day trial ending

Thursday afternoon, after which everybody except Redman would go home early. But we all forgot one thing." He paused, and then in his best Baltimore accent said, "We were in Bawlmer, Hon. And the only thing you can count on in Baltimore, other than Old Bay Seasoning, Burger Cookies, and the Orioles breaking your heart is that you can't count on anything."

"So what went south?"

"South, hell, Grace, it went all the way down to the Keys and slapped Jimmy Buffett in the face. The trial went the way it was supposed to. The jury impaneled in a day. Nice looking bunch, nice variety. One young guy, the rest middle-aged or older. You know, the kind that don't take stuff from anybody. ASA Lawrence put on a good case. Defense was a woman named O'Connell. She made the usual objections, asked the usual questions. She didn't have much to work with and when she tried to attack the validity of DNA and the fingerprint and firearms matches Devereux shut her down. She rested without putting on any witnesses. Apparently, nobody liked Redman enough to give him a fake alibi. It went to the jury Wednesday afternoon and went to Hell Thursday morning."

Don looked at his watch. "I'm not keeping you, am I?"

I shook my head. It was a Saturday before noon. There hadn't been good cartoons on in the mornings for decades and I had no place to go. My wife Linda was the manager of the Baltimore Albion in Baltimore's Inner Harbor East. This weekend she was at a convention in a Philadelphia hotel, talking about hotels. So, no, Don wasn't keeping me and he clearly needed to talk.

I shook my head. "Not as long as you're buying the coffee and the cinnamon rolls."

"Ask any sheriff's deputy assigned to the courtrooms. It's nothing to hear shouting coming out of the jury room during deliberations. People have strong emotions. People are people and they have strong feelings about justice, racism, sexism, guilt, innocence, the police, whatever. Some can't stand to be disagreed with, and some people can't stand people like that. I had an uncle who thought that the louder he talked the more convincing he was. Bill Perry was the deputy on duty in Part 3, and he told me later that this didn't seem like a shouting case. But come Friday morning …"

Don goes on to tell me that, according to Perry, the jury assembled at nine and were in the room by nine-fifteen. The shouting started about ten – two people, loud enough to be heard through the door. The deputies have strict rules – nobody goes into the jury room unless someone shouts for help or hits the emergency alarm. So Perry just sat at his table and waited for reason to be restored.

It got quiet. Then the screaming started. Perry rushed in to find eleven jurors standing on one side of the room and another one on the floor on the opposite side. That one was dead.

"Believe it or not," Don told me, "the Sheriff's Department has a procedure for something like this. Perry checked and made sure that the guy on the floor was dead. He was. Then he asked if anyone else was injured. No takers. Then he told them all to be quiet, planted himself in front of the door, and called it in."

Don took a break for more coffee and another roll. I got a fill-up but passed on the roll. One a day was enough for me, according to my wife that is. After taking a bite and savoring the flavor of cinnamon mixed with icing, Don went on with his tale of woe.

"Lucky me, being involved in the case I was already there, hanging outside of Part 3 waiting for the verdict. So I got the call. I went in and another deputy led me to the jury room where I walked right into what we call a WWPD moment."

"What would Parker do?"

"Damn straight. I did know that the last thing he'd want me to do is ask, 'What happened'?"

"Why? Isn't that the whole point of an investigation?"

"Yeah, Grace, but what if one of them had said, 'I killed him.' I would have questioned him without reading him his rights, the confession gets suppressed, and the whole case gets tossed."

"So did you make Parker proud?"

"I think so. I told them to listen up then I read them their rights, with Perry there as my witness. When I asked if anybody wanted to remain silent or to talk to a lawyer I got no takers. I'm sure at least one of them wanted to invoke but was afraid to be separated from the herd. Who knows what the rest would have said about them?

"Then I checked on the victim. It was the young guy. From the looks of things, it was a push and fall, his head hitting the table edge as he went down. And that was all she wrote.

"Any of them could have done it. A heated argument, a few pushes, and then you've got a murder scene.

"I looked them over. You know I never bought into that thing about people looking guilty. Some of the jurors did and some didn't but there were none of them I'd put money on. So, their rights having been read, I asked what happened and who had done it."

"None of them spoke up, but most of them looked at this guy Malcolm Powers. But you can't make an arrest on a few looks. Not anymore."

Don smiled as if thinking about the good ole, bad ole days that all the veterans had told him about.

"I really didn't want to take them all down to the office, give them time to think on the ride over because nobody wants to be a witness in a murder case, especially not when it involves some poor bastard who had lost his temper for just a moment. I'd get eleven different versions of 'I didn't see a thing, my head was turned when it happened.' The room wasn't that big for all of them not to have seen anything, but which ones truly didn't see and which were lying?

"So I rolled the dice. I walked up to Malcolm and asked, 'Is there something you'd like to tell me, Sir, or do I arrest everybody here as accessories after the fact'?"

"You can do that?" I asked Don.

He shook his head. "Probably not, but they didn't know that. What they did know was that the only thing worse than being a witness in a murder case is being a defendant. As soon as I said this there were three fingers pointing at Malcolm and three versions of 'He did it'."

"I again asked Malcolm if he had anything to say and this time he took a breath and gave it up.

"'They all were ready to convict without talking about it. I had questions I wanted to ask before sending this young man away for life. You know, about coincidences, and planted evidence, and what that lady lawyer said about fingerprints and such not being reliable'."

"'The judge said we weren't supposed to consider that,' said one woman.

"'Well I wanted to,' Malcolm almost shouted. I thought he was going to go for her but instead his shoulders just slumped and he said, 'Next thing I knew Dennis and me were shouting and then I pushed him and then …' Malcolm sat down. There were tears in his eyes when he said, 'I didn't mean to, I wasn't supposed to …' He had said enough but might have said more when that same woman said,

"'It was Malcolm who started it, like he meant to start a fight. And it looked like he deliberately pushed Dennis, like he'd made up his mind.'

"I'd gotten enough. It was downtown and statement time. And that was that. Another dunker on the board in black. But it was yesterday that was the bitch."

"What happened?" I asked.

"Baltimore happened, Grace. The case of State vs. Boles Redman resumed Friday. ASA Lawrence made a motion to continue Monday with the ten remaining jurors. Before PD O'Connell could object Devereux told Lawrence that it was a nice try but since the case had already gone to the jury and since the remaining jurors had been compromised, she had no choice but to declare a mistrial. Then she added that jeopardy had attached and that the case against Redman was dismissed. We had just lost a dunker."

Don again looked at his watch. "Look, I got to get in. Parker wants us to put together something for the Feds, maybe get Redman indicted on federal charges. Hey, thanks for letting me vent. It's good to talk to somebody who used to be there."

Yeah, "used to be" was right. Ten years as a CSI and more as a private investigator and now I pushed papers for the State's Attorney Office. It wasn't the most exciting job, but I had steady money coming in, an eight-to-four schedule, and nobody shoots at me. Still, there are times …

What the hell, I thought, Linda's not going to be home until Monday afternoon. I ordered another cinnamon roll and thought about good luck and bad luck and wondered why they never seemed to balance.

Throughout the weekend, in between goofing off and taking care of the 'honey-do" list Linda had left me, I wondered about the Redman case. There was something about it that bothered me, something that was trying to wake up the PI I used to be. It wasn't until Sunday night when I was watching some movie I'd forget twenty minutes after it was over that some things Don had mentioned came back to me…

"I wasn't supposed to …"

"like he wanted to start a fight …"

"deliberately pushed Dennis …"

No way, I thought as the idea started forming. Like the two Michael Jacksons theory, it sounded good but I just couldn't believe it. Still …

Having been a PI I knew how to find information most people, even these days, didn't have access to. It took me less than thirty minutes to find everything there was on Malcom Powers.

White male, 48, divorced with one child he couldn't see because he was behind on child support. Way behind. Of course, that might be due to the fact that he'd been unemployed for over a year. A few address changes, the last being to his brother's house. Yeah, he'd be my candidate.

I then thought about who had access to juror names – prosecution, defense (including the defendant), the court, the Jury Commissioner's Office. Even before the jury is picked they know your name, age, occupation, and level of education. I had less than that to go on and I had no problem finding Malcolm.

I called Don.

"What is it, Grace?"

"You owe me breakfast, no, make that lunch." Then I told him why.

"No way."

"Just call Devereux. She'll be up. From what I've heard, she watches late-night true crime shows with a human skull on her lap. Get a warrant for the brother's house and see how many gift cards you find. I'll bet you that lunch you owe me that they were bought at the same store Redman's payoff came from."

Don got the warrant and made his search. Then he called Central Booking. Once he had Malcolm back in the interview room, with his PD sitting next to him and Lieutenant Parker blocking the door like the Wrath of God (which in many ways he was), Don simply put two $2500 VISA gift cards on the table. (I found out later that they were purchased from the same store as the ones Redmond received.)

"Recognize these, Mr. Powers? You're looking at murder for hire and, given the circumstances, this one goes to the Feds. They still have the death penalty for things like this."

Don told me that before his lawyer could tell him to be quiet, Malcolm broke down. Guilt's a wonderful thing, isn't it? With tears rolling down his face, Malcolm said,

"I wasn't supposed to kill him, didn't mean to kill him. They just told me to pick a fight with somebody, hurt 'em just enough to get charged, so there'd be a mistrial and that jeopardy thing."

There was nothing more to say, not there, not then. The rest was between the State's Attorney's and the Public Defender's offices.

On Tuesday morning I thought it was all over except for me deciding where Don was taking me and Linda to dinner. I know, it was supposed to be lunch for two but Parker made Don give me an upgrade for doing his job for him. But like I said, I thought it was over but then Don called,

"Grace, Part 3, ten o'clock. Something's happening."

When I got to the courtroom I saw that Judge Devereux had brought all the principles of the State vs. Boles Redman back together. (Court orders and bench warrants are wonderful things.) ASA Lawrence looked confused. PD O'Connell was objecting loudly to "this abuse of judicial authority."

"I can abuse it more, Counselor. Did you bring a toothbrush? If not, I have one here in what I call my contempt gift bag." Her honor held up a small, black bag. "It has everything you'll need in lockup – toothbrush, toothpaste, deodorant, hand sanitizer, even a small roll of decent bathroom tissue."

O'Connell shut up and sat down as Devereux addressed the room.

"Information has come to me that has caused me to rethink my ruling on double jeopardy in this case. It seems that due to a conspiracy the defendant may not have been in jeopardy at all. So I'm reversing my ruling. Do sit down, Ms. O'Connell. Save it for the Courts of Appeal. Now unless you all want to work things out here and now, we can set a trial date."

ASA Lawrence was quick. "Ten years, Mr. Redman, Ms. O'Connell, and I won't file murder for hire charges on this death or Dennis Monroe's."

"You can't prove my client's involvement."

"I'm willing to try. Ten years?"

"Eight years."

"Why don't we let Her Honor decide?"

There was an anticipatory gleam in Devereux's eyes that no one in the courtroom, least of all O'Connell, missed. Not wishing to roll the dice, she had a brief, whispered conference with her client and, at his nod, said, "Ten years."

A quick plea later and Boles Redman was sentenced as per the plea agreement. On his way out, Judge Devereux stopped him.

"Here, Mr. Redman," she said, handing him the black bag, "you'll be needing this."

Dinner at Bowman's Restaurant was excellent. Parker even joined us, paying his own way and kicking in for drinks.

"So what's going to happen to Mr. Powers," Linda asked over cheesecake.

Don answered her. "Involuntary manslaughter, sentence to be determined by anyone other than Judge Devereux. And he doesn't get to keep the gift cards."

MISSING ... PRESUMED

It took a few weeks, but the sensationalism of the courthouse murder of Judge Phillip Hanover by his lover finally faded from the news. But if word ever leaked out about the nude photos Judge Hanover took of his former lovers, the media would again catch fire.

After solving the judge's murder, I went back to my regular job as Chief Forensic Investigator for Baltimore's State's Attorney's Office. One day, if the SAO ever loosens their purse strings, they may hire someone for me to be chief over but for now it's just me, reviewing photographs and forensic reports from the BPD's Laboratory Division and recommending further action and analyses where needed. Mostly this was requesting DNA profiles in cases where the primary officer or detective had failed to do so or asking the investigator to follow-up on fingerprint IDs to determine if the prints belonged to the defendant, the victim, a family member, or a collateral bystander. It's a necessary but not exciting job but it does get me home at a decent hour each night and my weekends are usually free.

So there I was, in my closet of an office, happily reading reports, looking at crime scene photographs, and making sure that what I read matched what I saw. That's when my office phone rang. It was my immediate boss, Deputy State's Attorney Sharon Manchester.

"Matthew," she said, "drop what you're doing. You need to see Celina as soon as possible."

"I saw enough of Celina on Hanover's hard drive. Tell me, did she claim his chair after the crime scene was released. She looked so ... comfortable in it."

Yes, Baltimore City's State's Attorney was one of those who had posed for Judge Hanover. Sharon and I pretend we didn't see her photos and I wouldn't think of mentioning it to her (okay, I'd think about it but never do it) or using it against her in any way unless she came at me first.

"Knock it off and go see her. She has a job for you."

"I have a job."

"Another job. She'll explain."

Ten minutes later I was in Celina Alston's office. Top floor, great view of the Inner Harbor. A power office for a power player.

Celina Alston was the latest in a long line of Alstons. Her family went back to 1890 when Baltimore's City Council was made up of two branches. It's been rumored that the Alstons were part of a secret third branch that ran the city. It's also rumored that the Third Branch still exists. If so, Alston is probably a member, or very much wants to be.

Alston has the kind of blue-eyed, blond hair good looks that lead to either politics or an anchor position on the evening news. Being an overachiever, Alston went for the double. She started out on the local news and worked her way up to the big desk. After a few years of leading with "breaking news," she used her popularity and her law degree to get elected as Baltimore's State's Attorney, despite never having tried a case outside of District Court. Once she gets tired of running the SAO she'll probably try for mayor.

She's been "campaigning" for that office since she got her anchor position. Whenever there was a police scandal or an officer-involved shooting or an in-custody death, she personally reported on it. She became the on-air crusader against police behaving badly in Baltimore and the surrounding counties. She used this persona to get herself elected and now takes every opportunity to put cops in jail.

Mostly I have no problem with that. I helped do the same back when I worked crime scenes and later as a private investigator. But Alston went past holding bad cops accountable and lapsed into overzealousness. That her efforts have led to a plateful of acquittals and an officer being sent to prison for a murder he didn't commit doesn't seem to bother her constituents. They see her as their champion, and I can't honestly say they're wrong. That's her job. I just wish she wouldn't break the law while doing it.

Alston doesn't like me as much I don't like her. She rightly suspects my involvement in exonerating the above-mentioned police officer. But I'm useful to her. My forensic reviews often suggest analyses that either strengthen or save cases. That leads to convictions and those convictions might lead her to City Hall. I expect that one day she'll fire me or I'll resign. Until then, it's a matter of "keep your enemy close" for both of us.

When I walked into Alston's office I was surprised not to find Ogden Manners, her top deputy, with her. Manners is her combined stooge and hitman, doing the dirty work she can't be seen doing. For a brief time, he was a suspect in Judge Hanover's murder and my home safe holds a piece of paper that involves him in evidence tampering and obstruction of justice.

It was just the two of us and that was good. If she were going to fire me, she'd have at least one witness and a security guard who would hand me a cardboard box and escort me first to my office and then to Baltimore Street. I knew that this was going to be interesting.

"Please sit down, Grace." I did and she went on. "Have you heard of The Brays?"

Sensing that this was not the time or place to make a donkey joke, I gave her my straight answer. "Who hasn't? Victoria and Nicholas Bray. They're in the papers and on the news at least every other week. They seem to be good people. Or at the least, they haven't been caught being naughty, despite *The Baltimore Truth's* best efforts." I left out the rumors of mob connections. There are always such rumors about the wealthy and successful since people can't believe that they didn't become or stay successful or wealthy without outside help.

"We all have our naughty side, Grace." Was that a dare or a brag? The slight smile that crossed her face didn't give me an answer. "Nick and Vicky have a daughter. Janis is Vicky's child by her first marriage although Nick treats her like his own."

"How did her natural father treat her?" Alston looked surprised. "This is about the girl, right? Otherwise, you wouldn't have mentioned her."

Alston gave me another look then a nod. "You're wasted in that office of yours, Grace."

"So I've been told, but I like the hours and the quiet. Now about Janis … does she go by Bray or her birth father's name?"

"Bray, Nick adopted her. Her birth father abused both her and Vicky. Vicky physically, Janis mentally, He would beat Vicky and, well, do other things to her in front of their daughter. Things ended … badly."

The case came back to me. Stan Gregory was a wife-beater who one night finally turned on his daughter. Before he could lay a hand, or anything else, on Janis, Victoria hit him with something hard and heavy and made herself a window. No charges were filed and after a few years and some therapy, Victoria met and married Nicholas Bray. I was a PI at the time and when I heard I about it on the news I was glad not to have been involved.

"Ms. Alston," I said in the tone of voice I once used on my clients, "tell me the problem with Janis."

I expected to be told that Janis Bray was involved with drugs, or had been assaulted in some way, or something else crime-related. This would be followed by Alston asking me to expedite any forensic reports. So I was surprised to hear, "She's missing."

Missing? That was it? The BPD had an entire unit for that. Why was I needed? I didn't say this, of course. Instead, I asked, "What kind of missing?"

Alston gave it to me straight. Three weeks ago, Janis went on a trip, supposedly to New York City, supposedly with a few of her girlfriends. She was an independent type and not one to call home more than once a week unless she needed something. The week went by without her calling. A few days later Victoria started calling her, leaving messages. No answer. After two weeks, Nicholas called one of his business contacts in New York, who called an NYPD deputy chief. The chief called the Brays and a missing person report was filed.

"And since I'm here in your office with you telling me about this, the NYPD did not find her."

"They found nothing except that her phone hadn't pinged

anywhere in their city. Its last location being just outside Pennsylvania Station, the one here in Baltimore, not the one in New York."

"Has she done this before, gone off on a trip and stayed away for weeks without contact?"

"Yes on the trips, no on the 'without contact.' She might not have phoned home but she was very active on the social sites, constantly posting about where she was and what she was doing."

"And no posts from the train to or from NYC? No photos of an overpriced Belgium Waffle at the Brooklyn Diner, or shots of her in Bryant Park, with a cow statue in Central Park, or whatever young women take pictures of these days." Alston shook her head. "And her parents didn't notice this?"

"Janis blocked her parents from all her sites."

There were ways around that. Sitting there in front of Alston's too neat, too clean desk I could think of at least three. As a parent (which I'm not but Linda and I are happily working on it) I'd use at least one of them. Hey, it's not prying or an invasion of privacy if you don't get caught.

"Since her last known location – correction, her phone's last known location was here in Baltimore, have the Brays called the BPD to report her missing?"

Alston huffed. (There's no other word for the noise that came out of her). "For all the good it did. It's all in here."

She handed me a very thin folder that contained a printout of the BPD investigation. A glance showed that it was a typical report for this kind of incident. An of-age adult goes missing. No signs of any foul play. Write it, file it, forget it, move on to the higher-profile cases. In a town that consistently makes the "top five" list of the most dangerous cities in America, that's standard practice.

Except for the rich, the privileged, and the well-connected.

"Ms. Alston, forgive me for saying this, but with your contacts in City Hall, the State House, and the news media, and with Nicholas Bray's connections to, well, just about everyone of importance, you two have enough influence to call on the full force of the BPD, the Maryland State Police, and possibly the FBI to investigate this. So why me? I'm just a forensic investigator."

"You're more than that. Judge Deveraux thought so and your … discrete solving of Judge Hanover's murder proved it. And as of now, I'm making it official." She handed me an important looking letter. "You're now a special investigator for this office. You'll continue with your regular duties unless you're needed on more important matters. And you'll need this."

She handed me a badge and all the power and responsibility that came with it. I thought to refuse it, but I didn't have to use or carry it. Like the gun that came with it.

I looked at my promotion notice and saw that it came with a decent pay raise. So I decided to take it. I'd probably wind up doing the job anyway so I might as well have the title and the money.

But that didn't answer my question.

"Thank you, Ms. Alston. But again, why me?"

"The Brays and I are close. They supported my election campaign and donated heavily to it. From that, we became personal friends. It was as their friend that I suggested we do just what you said. Fearing the publicity, they declined. They want this matter handled quietly. That's when I offered the services of this office, that is, you."

"To do what?"

"To find their daughter and probably solve her murder."

I thought that a bit dramatic. Then I thought again. If Alston suspected the Brays, she'd cover things up before involving me. That meant,

"Janis had a boyfriend. One that her parents didn't like."

Alston nodded. "She'd had some casual relationships in the past – a few boys in high school, one or two in college before she dropped out. It was she who ended them all. But this one, with this Morgan Uris, was serious."

Morgan Uris. I'd heard or read the name before but could not remember where or when. Holmes would have remembered, so would Archie Goodwin. The latter would have told Nero Wolfe who would have solved the case before it was time to tend his orchids.

"Morgan? Male or female?"

"Male."

An abusive father. Casual relationships that led nowhere. This one was serious and now Janis is missing. No wonder Alston and probably the Bray's are thinking murder. That led me to ask,

"Any signs of abuse."

Alston wasn't startled by my question. I suspect that if I hadn't asked she would have brought it up. "What makes you ask that?"

I almost said, "Elementary, my dear Alston," but instead I shook my head.

"I've heard this story before, mostly when I was in private practice. Usually, it was the parents who came to me, occasionally it was adult children worried about Mom or Dad. Sometimes it was the victims themselves, wanting out of a dangerous situation. I helped some of them but other times things ended … badly. And I see it in my current job, reviewing CSU photos and reports from domestic violence cases. The same faces, sometimes the same abusers, sometimes new ones. Like drugs, it's a social problem as much as a police …"

Reports, police … I remembered where I'd heard the name Morgan Uris before.

"Uris is a cop, isn't he?"

"Yes, he is. They met about nine, ten months ago. He pulled her over for DUI. She batted her eyes and flashed some cleavage but he followed procedure. Towed her car and brought her in for a breath test. When she failed he decided that discretionary release was in order and let her call her parents to pick her up."

"And she still went out with him?"

"Officer Uris failed to appear for the MVA hearing and Janis got her license back. Then he failed to appear for court at her trial and all charges were dismissed. A month later Uris and Janis began seeing each other."

Given Alston's bias against the police, I could see why she was thinking abuse and murder. But thinking it doesn't make it real.

"Signs of abuse?" I prompted.

"Other than a sprained wrist about a month ago, none. At least, none that showed. Maybe under her clothes. Or maybe it's mental, or … sexual."

Alston paused, sighed, then, "Vicky should have called me. She'd been through it all herself. She should have called as soon as she suspected something. I would have checked up on him. Why didn't she call?"

Up until now, I had seen Celina Alston as my boss and not a very good one, someone willing to sacrifice others for her political agenda. Now she was human, worried for her friend, asking herself what she could have done and feeling guilty about not doing anything to fix a problem she didn't know about.

Still, her small display of humanity did not grant her pardon for her sins. It just showed that there was some good in everyone.

I asked Alston the usual questions. Credit and debit card activity, cash withdrawals, her friends.

"The Missing Persons Unit did do that right, at least the banking. No card or online activity, $5,000 cash withdrawal two days before she left. As for her friends, the ones her parents knew about weren't aware of any trip."

"About this Uris?"

"I checked. He's been on duty every day since she left. Either working patrol or secondary employment security. If she's alive, he's not with her."

Unless she's shacked up at his place, I thought.

"Her car?"

"Still at her house. Her parents weren't home when she left so they have no idea how she got to the station."

Cab or rideshare. Easy to check. That is, if she actually got to the station and not just her phone.

"Grace, Morgan Uris is a violent thug with a badge, one with multiple complaints of excessive force, some of which fit the legal definition of aggravated assault. You can check his record for yourself."

"And the outcomes of these complaints?"

"What you would expect from the BPD. Reports written by fellow officers justifying his use of force, failure to call CSU on the more serious cases, exoneration by Internal Affairs on all but one complaint with only a letter of reprimand on that one. And who knows how many unreported assaults there were?"

I could help her with that last one. "Request his body cam footage. Have it reviewed, all of it. It's a boring job so get someone whose last name is other than Grace to do it. If it shows him abusing his position or improperly turning off the camera, charge him."

At Alston's surprise, I added, "I don't like bad cops any more than you do, Ms. Alston. I just don't like it when good cops go to jail for something they didn't do."

There, I'd said it. I'd drawn the line then crossed it. If she asked for the badge back I'd give it to her then find myself a cardboard box. There was a minute or two of quiet as she no doubt tried to think of someone else who could the job with the skill and discretion she needed. Finally, she said, "So noted."

A truce then, so back to work. "What do you think happened and why do you think it might be murder?"

"I don't know. Maybe he didn't want her to go. It got physical and she finally fought back. He hit her too hard and killed her. He took her phone to Penn Station so it would look like she'd been there. Or maybe he offered to drive her there and took her someplace else. But if he killed her, as a trained officer he knew how to clean up a crime scene. He'd probably done it before in some of those aggravated excessive force cases. He'd also know how and where to dispose of a body. I'm trusting you to be better than he is, Grace. If Janis Bray is alive or dead, find her. If she's dead, prove that he did it."

"No, Ma'am."

The look she gave me made me wonder if anyone had ever said "No" to her before, especially in this office. Before she could say anything like, "You're fired, get out" I said,

"I'll look for Janis Bray up to the limit of my abilities. If I can't find her, you or her parents will have to use those connections I talked about. If I find her alive, great. If I find her body or proof that's she dead then it becomes a police matter. I will not manufacture evidence just to put a certain person in prison."

Actually, I had done just that on several occasions, one of those occasions leading to my abrupt departure from the BPD. But that was long ago and I'm a much better person now. Or so I tell myself. And on those occasions when I don't want to listen to me, I think of the people who believe that I am – Linda, Sharon, Lieutenant Parker. There's no way I'd want to disappoint any of them.

"Perhaps I misspoke, Grace. What I meant to say was that if Janis is dead, I expect you to find her killer, whoever it is. But if it is Uris …"

"Whoever it is, I'll nail their hide to the wall and bring you their head on a pike."

"That's all I ask, Grace."

Maybe Alston was reluctant to involve the BPD, but she did not specifically tell me not to. When I got back to my office, I called the Missing Persons Unit, which, due to budget cuts and an ever-increasing crime rate, was down to three people: a sergeant, an officer, and an admin clerk who also did the payroll for most of the Criminal Investigation Division. With only two investigators, no wonder that for them it's mostly file, make some calls, and forget.

I reached out to the MPU sergeant, Maurice Richardson. "Yes, Grace, what can I do you for?"

"Just a heads up, Sarge. Do you remember taking a missing report on Janis Bray?"

The phone was silent for a time then, "Yeah, a few days ago. Young, in her early twenties, no sign of foul play, last location the train station. We made the usual calls to hospitals and the Medical Examiners, sent out the usual alerts, marked it pending, and went back to looking for missing kids. Lots of them in Charm City. I'd like to ask officers to make nice with the squeegee kids while their body cams are running just to see if I get any matches. "

"Good idea, why don't you?"

"Because the same assholes who say they care about these kids complained that cops talking to them could be considered harassment and recording them was an invasion of their privacy. But anyway, what's with the Bray broad? Wait a minute, you're still working for Her, aren't you?"

Non-command members of the BPD do not mention Alston by name. They hate her that much.

"Unfortunately, yes. Needs must when the devil drives and I need to eat."

"You've made a deal with the devil alright. Let me guess. She's friends with the Brays and now it's a red ball."

"Just slightly pink for now, Sarge. But I just wanted to let you know that it could go red at any time. And by the way, She doesn't know I'm calling you, so let's put down any further steps you take to your initiative and due diligence. And if you do find her before I do you'll have the thanks of a very powerful Baltimore family."

"Thanks, Grace, you're a good guy. You might be in bed with Her, but at least you don't know where all her scars, moles, and tattoos are."

Little did he know.

Thanks to my warning, Peterson would probably personally contact hospitals and police agencies outside the Baltimore area, maybe into DC and the surrounding states. In a few days, he'd let me know what he found – good, bad, or nothing at all. At my suggestion, he said that he'd check with the cab and rideshare companies.

With Missing Persons doing some of my work for me, I started my own search.

I decided to work on the presumption that Janis was still alive, that she was somewhere off the grid either voluntarily or otherwise. After all, it's easier to find a live person than a dead one. So many places to hide a body in and around Baltimore, not to mention all the places within a five-hour drive. Lots of caverns in Virginia – some open to tourists, some on private grounds, some unexplored. I wonder how many calcium-covered bodies are slowly turning into stalagmites.

I would have to pay some attention to Morgan Uris. I wasn't ready to declare Janis "missing – presumed dead" but if the presumption bore out he'd be the prime suspect.

I called the Brays to make an appointment for the next day to talk to them and search Janis's room. Ms. Bray took the call and said that she would be glad to see me but that her husband would be busy at work.

"Does Mr. Bray work in the area?" He did, she admitted. "Then surely he can't be too busy to help me find your daughter?"

There was a brief silence, then she put me on hold. After a few minutes of Vivaldi's *Mandolin Concerto in C Major* Victoria came back on the line.

"Nicholas will be here," she said in a harsh tone that made me wonder if she was mad at me, her husband, or both of us.

As soon as I broke the connection my phone rang. (Okay, it wasn't as much a ring as the theme from The Batman TV show.) I had a brief hope that it was Sarge Peterson telling me that Janis had been found but no, it was Ogden Manners calling to tell me that some unlucky interns had been given the job of reviewing the body camera footage of "randomly selected patrol officers" and that Uris was first on the list. The footage would go back sixty days. If Uris was behaving badly on camera he deserved whatever he got.

I'd have to talk to him of course. He was the boyfriend, he might know where she was or might have gone. But he was also a cop and knew that in these cases we might be thinking murder and might be thinking about him. I'd need ammunition.

I went to my computer, typed in a username and a password that I should not have had, and pulled up Morgan Uris's service record.

The last thing I did before going home that evening was to arrange a meeting with Judge Cordelia Copper. Her pictures had also been on Judge Hanover's laptop, although unlike most of his subjects she had not known she was being photographed and recorded.

The next morning I was explaining the situation to the judge, telling her that I may soon need some warrants signed. I asked for advice on what she would consider probable cause in these circumstances. I did not ask this of Judge Copper because of the photographs. As far as I knew, she still wasn't aware of them. No, I asked her because she was one of the few judges to whose reelection campaign the Brays had not contributed.

"I ruled against his company in a civil matter. This was his way of showing his displeasure. From what I've heard, he's somewhat of a vindictive man."

She smiled at my, "But you won anyway."

Copper shrugged. "I was on the slate, and the slate almost always wins."

"But given his lack of support, you would not be inclined to grant a warrant involving his family that was not properly written and without merit."

"And if I turned the warrant down it would appear as if I was every bit as vindictive as Mr. Bray."

"Not at all, Your Honor. Your turning it down would not leave these chambers. But the reason I've come to you today is to seek your advice so that does not happen."

That must have been the right answer because she said, "Gertrude Deveraux mentioned that you probably majored in BS in college. She also said that you were discrete and could be trusted." She gave me a smile that told me that Judge Deveraux had spilled the beans. "When and if the time comes see me. But make sure you have something I can sign with a reasonably clear conscience."

"Thank you, Your Honor."

Victoria and Nicholas Bray received me warmly at their Guilford home. That is, she did. He seemed put out at having to help me find his missing daughter. He tried to be subtle about it but he kept checking his watch as if he had someplace more important to be. Maybe he did. Maybe, despite his adopting her, Mr. Bray never considered Janis as his daughter but just part of the package deal that came with his marrying Victoria.

I could see why he took the deal. Victoria Bray was elegantly beautiful with a core of strength that shone through her. I could see that what she had suffered at the hands of her first husband had not broken but strengthened her. The therapy simply put the finishing touches on what she had already become.

Nicholas Bray looked every bit the modern-day business

owner. He was wearing a suit that cost more than all of mine put together – and he wore it well. He had the kind of good looks that would carry him into his late sixties, early seventies before he truly started to show his age. And when he talked, moved, or even sat he did so with the attitude that he was the most important, the most powerful person in the room.

Maybe he was, in his world. And maybe Ms. Bray ruled things at home. But we were in my world now and its most important person wasn't in the room. She was out there somewhere, missing and possibly dead, and it was my job to find her and their job to help me.

I started asking them the same questions I had asked Alston. Bray interrupted me with, "Didn't your boss tell you all of this?"

Patience, I told myself. Maybe he's worried about his missing daughter and his attitude is just his way of not showing how worried he was in front of her mother. Or maybe he's just anxious to get to wherever I was keeping him from.

Which is a bad attitude to have when being questioned. It only makes people like me start to wonder where he'd rather be. I wrote a reminder in the notebook I was using to find out where that was.

I tried not to let anything show. Instead, I gave him the detective's smile of reassurance and said,

"Yes, she did. But what Ms. Alston told me was secondhand, hearsay if you will. I'd like to get it direct from the two of you to make sure nothing was left out, no matter how trivial. Sometimes it's the little things that lead to the truth of the matter."

Bray had more to say but his wife stopped him with "We understand, Mr. Grace. Please, ask as many questions as you like."

So I went over it all again. I learned nothing new. Ms. Bray had some recent photos of Janis on her phone which she sent to me. I got a list of Janis's friends, the ones the Brays knew about, and their phone numbers. I even got contact info on two ex-boyfriends that Janis had brought home to meet the folks. I'd have to ask the girlfriends about those. Maybe one of her exes still resented the breakup.

When I finished with my questions Bray all but jumped from

his chair asking, "Is that all?"

"For now, Mr. Bray. I may have more at a later time." At this, he turned and left the room without a "thank you" or a "goodbye."

Ms. Bray was not the kind of woman who felt it necessary to apologize or explain her husband's actions. His sins were his alone as long as he didn't commit them against her.

"Will there be anything else, Mr. Grace?"

"Yes, Ma'am. May I please see Janis's room." With a smile, I added, "You can stay and watch me if you like."

"I don't think that will be necessary. Celina would not have sent you if she didn't trust you. So I suppose I can trust you as well. Let me take you up."

When we got to Janis's room I asked, "Other than the clothes she packed for the trip, is there anything missing from this room?"

Ms. Bray paled slightly, and I saw the first crack in the wall she had built to keep her own worries away. "I must confess, Mr. Grace, that I could not tell you. I'm afraid I don't know my daughter as well as I should. Maybe that's my fault, maybe it's hers, maybe both. But it's as if she mentally moved out when she turned eighteen. Maybe if I had …"

She did not need to go there. "What-ifs" will kill you every time.

"Children grow up," I said quietly, "and then they grow apart. There's nothing any parent can do about that."

I don't know if that helped but she gave me a quick smile of thanks and said, "I'll leave you to your work."

I did a thorough search of Janis's room. There were no empty areas from which things had been removed. No large gaps in her wardrobe not explained by packing for a trip. At the bottom of her closet, which was only slightly smaller than the guest room in my house, was a set of matched luggage. It was light blue with dark blue stripes. A check of the brand and model number showed that it was a six-piece set. Only five pieces were in the closet. The largest piece was gone. Janis had not traveled light.

There was no phone in her room, neither the one that pinged at the train station or any other. There were no papers, notes, photographs, event tickets, or receipts. There were no books to rifle through. I was not surprised. These days a lot of people do everything online. Which brought me to her computer.

It was on her desk that was against the one wall that did not have a window. It was a laptop, maybe a year old. Despite packing heavy, she didn't take it with her. Maybe she thought she wouldn't need it, that she'd use her phone. The phone which may or may not be at Penn Station.

Thoughts of phones and computers reminded me of a question I had forgotten to ask. Picking up the laptop, I left the room to find Ms. Bray.

She was in the living room, quietly drinking coffee and maybe thinking about the stranger who was rifling through her daughter's underwear drawer. And yes, I had, but there was nothing I hadn't seen too many times in the ransacked bedrooms of burglary victims. And no, I didn't find anything that might help me locate Janis.

"Ms. Bray," I said, interrupting whatever she was thinking.

"Yes, Mr. Grace?" When she stood and faced me I saw that her eyes were red. She pretended they weren't and I pretended not to notice.

"I'm going to need to take Janis's laptop. There may be something on it that will help me find her. I'll give you a receipt or it."

As I was writing out the receipt I asked the question I had forgotten.

"Ms. Alston said that Janis had blocked you and Mr. Bray from her social media sites. Did she give you any reason?"

The look on her face showed me that I opened an old wound but she just shook her head and said, "She told us before she did it. Said that she didn't want us 'prying' into her life, 'spying' on her. That if we needed to know something we could ask."

"And did you and Mr. Bray discuss a, well, workaround?"

She knew what I meant. "Nicholas suggested doing just that, said he had people working for him that could access the sites. I insisted we respect her privacy. She went through so much as a child, invading her privacy seemed to me as a kind of assault."

"I think you made the proper and decent choice, Ms. Bray." Then I handed her the receipt, effectively telling her that I would be invading Janis's privacy in the most extreme way.

I thanked her, she thanked me, and I left. There was time before lunch to go to Penn Station.

Flashing the badge I never thought I'd use, I went down to the arrivals and departures platform of Penn Station and watched people get on and off the trains. Most of them carried small to medium-sized bags although there were some with full-sized cases. I asked the platform security officer about this.

He shrugged. "The overheads are large enough. The trick is getting them up there. If you can't lift the weight you shouldn't travel heavy."

I thought this good advice even for people who might never get on a train. Then I thought about Janis. While more than medium height, from her photos she didn't seem to have the upper body strength needed to lift her large suitcase to the overhead. Maybe I was wrong, there's a lot you can't tell from a photograph, maybe she could have lifted and thrown it up there. Of course, with her being young and attractive, I'm sure there were several men and maybe some women who would be glad to help her get it up and down.

Then the dark part of my mind kicked in, the part every investigator needs if they're to be good at their job, that little voice that asks, "What if?"

A young woman on a train. A friendly guy comes up, helps her with her carry-on. He gets her talking. When it's time to leave, he gets her bag down and, "How about some coffee or lunch?" She says yes. He gets her coffee with something extra in it and soon he's got a new girl for his stable.

I wondered if a field trip to NYC was in order. Talk to security at its Penn Station, see if that had ever happened. While I was there, I'd get in touch with the Deputy Chief Nicholas Bray had talked to.

Doing this would take a day or two. I'd have to stay over. Of course, I'd bring Linda with me. Maybe the concierge at Linda's hotel could get us a comped room at the New York Albion, maybe even score us two tickets to *Hamilton.*

It was a nice thought but I could not imagine Alston going for it. I'd have to settle for making some phone calls. Maybe when this case was over it would be a way for Linda and me to celebrate my raise and promotion, assuming I solved the case and still had a job.

Between arrivals and departures, I asked platform security about my "helpful stranger" scenario. He allowed that it was possible but had never heard about it happening. I thanked him and went upstairs to the Lost and Found Department.

Like most things these days, Penn Station's Lost and Found is mostly online. I used my badge to find Gladys Smith, who was in charge of Lost and Found. She led me to the storage room and showed me where the phones were.

There were twelve of them. Janis's was one of them, the newest and most expensive one there. It had been found on one of the long wooden benches in the main lobby waiting area.

"Nice phone," Gladys said, "I'm surprised someone turned it in. I guess there are still some honest people in this world."

"Did you see who see who it was?" I asked, wondering if the honest person was a cop named Uris.

"No, it was in the L&F bin when I came in," she looked at the tag, "about three weeks ago. Anybody could have taken it in."

"I'll need to take it, State's Attorney's Investigation."

She gave me the phone, I gave her a receipt. "What if the owner comes back for it?" Gladys asked.

"I hope to hell she does," I said. I gave her one of my cards. "Have her call me if that happens."

Before leaving Penn Station there was one more thing to do. Starting at the bottom, I walked the down-under long term parking garage breathing in gas fumes and hoping not to smell the odor of a three-week-old body. I knew of three cases where bodies had been found in trunks in this garage and was hoping not to find a fourth in a dusty car. I got my wish.

Lunch then back to work. Sharon met me outside my office and congratulated me on my promotion.

"Are you still my boss?" I asked.

"Mostly, except for the dirty deeds Celina's going to have you do." She peeked into my office. "You're probably in line for a bigger one."

I shook my head. "I like this one, I know where everything is." And where the hiding places are. I should, I made them myself after Ogden Manners took all but one of my digital storage devices.

"Okay, but be careful, Matthew."

Why does everybody keep telling me that?

After three weeks, both Janis's cell and laptop were out of power. I scrounged the right charging cords and plugged them in. They'd be ready to go when I got back to work. I made some case-related calls, then went back to my other job of reviewing reports and photographs until it was quitting time.

"I want my FOP rep present."

Those were the first words out of Morgan Uris's mouth when I walked into the SAO meeting room where he had been waiting. The day before I had called his district's Admin Lieutenant and requested Uris's presence. When the lieutenant started talking about "backed-up service requests" and "patrol shortages" I cut him off with, "Fine, I'll have my boss call your boss. Who's your major?"

The lieutenant quickly answered with, "How about eight-thirty? Just don't keep him too long."

I responded to Morgan's demand with, "And I want an oceanfront condo in Ocean City overlooking a clothing-optional beach. But it's not a day for getting what we want."

I let that sink in for a moment then, "Tell me about you and Janis Bray."

The look on his face told me that whatever he was expecting the State's Attorney's Office to ask him, Janis Bray was not a part of it. It made me wonder what sins he had committed that he hoped we didn't know about.

"What about her?"

The two of them had been hot and heavy for several months and that was the best he could do?

"She's been missing for three weeks. You two were an item. I'll ask you straight. Do you know where she went or why she can't be found?"

"Missing?" He looked surprised, whether he really was was open to debate. "I didn't know. After our last couple of dates, I thought she'd ghosted me." Then it hit him. "Wait a damn minute … The Brays, that bitch Alston, you. You're fitting me up for this, aren't you?"

"For what, Officer Uris? As far as anyone knows, Janis is missing, not dead. You were her lover. It's standard procedure to interview those close to her. Now I'll ask again, did Janis give you any indication of where she was going or why she may not want to be found?"

"Go to Hell, you bastard." I'd heard that too many times. Points off for lack of originality. "Lawyer, FOP rep."

I gave Uris a "Well, I tried" shrug. "Okay, Officer, we're done with this matter. I'll just make a note that when you were informed about Janis Bray's disappearance you refused to help us find her."

Uris stood and in two words told me what I could do with myself. Then he told me I could do it to "that SAO bitch." More points off.

"Sit down, Officer," I ordered in my best Homicide Lieutenant voice. He sat right away, not knowing why. Thank you, Lieutenant Parker.

"I said that we were done with Janis Bray being missing. There's one other matter."

I handed him an accordion folder that was straining its pleats. "What this?"

"It's all your use of force reports and excessive force complaints over the last five years. You're on Alston's radar. She's considering presenting this…" I picked the folder then let it go. It hit the table with a thud. "… to the Grand Jury. She needs headlines and sound bites and she hasn't put a cop on trial for a while. Whether she does or not, well, that's up to me … and you."

If we hadn't been in the SAO's office, if he thought he could have gotten away with it, he might have shot me or slugged me. As it was, his face turned mean as he coldly said, "You mother-raper."

All points restored. Who would have thought that Uris had read Chester Himes?

I had Uris by the short and curlies and he knew it. If his file was presented to the Grand Jury they'd judge it by volume alone, thinking that where there's that much smoke something had to be on fire.

He sat back in his chair, not in defeat but in surrender to the inevitable. "What do you want to know?"

"For the record, Officer Uris, and to get the obvious out of the way, do you know where Janis Bray is?"

"No."

"Did you kill her?"

"No."

"Do you have any reason to believe that she's dead, either by accident or by her own hand or at the hand of another?"

"No."

"Okay then." He seemed surprised that I didn't follow-up on any of those questions. I had no reason to, there's was no evidence that she was dead, and if I had followed through, he might have lawyered up despite the accordion folder.

"Tell me about your last couple of dates."

He was relaxing, starting to believe that he was not a suspect. "Janis was always a fun girl. At first, it was just her being grateful for keeping her license and not getting a DUI on her record. And she was *very* grateful. I thought that once she … expressed her gratitude that would be all. But we hit it off. She liked being with a cop and listening to my stories, and I liked being with her. That she was great looking and rich didn't hurt. But, hey, I paid my way, where I could and when I could. She wanted to sit in the orchestra of the Hippodrome or to go to a steakhouse where the ribeye cost triple digits, that was on her. I covered most other places."

I nodded. I never had any problem with my dates treating. Now that we're married, Linda and I still take turns paying, even though it all comes out of the same checking account.

"Tell me about the last few times. What was she like?"

"Different, distant. Not as much fun. She didn't want to, you know, and she always wanted to do that. Off the record? Between me, you, and the table?"

"Yeah, sure."

"She loved, um, taking a ride in the back of the patrol car."

"But the last few times, no rides?" He shook his head. "Did she say what the problem was? Was anything worrying her?"

"I knew it was something, but she said it was nothing. And no, she didn't tell me what 'it' was."

"Did she tell you about her trip? Tell you where she was going?"

"New York City for a week, with some of her friends. Don't ask me which ones, I met them a few times, they seemed interchangeable. After she left, I tried calling her a few times but no luck. Tried again after she was supposed to come back. Finally, I decided that the 'it' was me. You can check on the phone calls, if you haven't already."

I hadn't but it was on my list.

With that, I told Uris that we were done, really done. The accordion folder wasn't mentioned. When he stood to leave he offered his hand saying, "You're okay, Grace. But your boss is still a bitch."

"No argument there," I said as he left.

Did I believe him? I'm on record as believing anyone for at least ten minutes. After that, well, except for God and Joshua Parker, everyone lies to everybody else, including themselves.

I would like to tell you that on finding Janis's phone locked that I did something forensically clever, such as after dusting her phone for prints and finding which four digits had been touched the most, I found that she had used the last four of her social security number, her phone number, or her birth year. Or that, having obtained a clear print from the drinking glass in her bathroom, I swiped it down the screen and the phone gave up its secrets. Or that it had a new feature. If you forgot your phone code, it would allow you to unlock it by texting UNLOCK three times from two different phones and that I had found this information on her laptop after hacking its entry password.

I'd like to tell you this but the reality is that despite what certain movies and TV shows will tell you, the first two won't work and the third, while a damned good idea, has yet to be developed or implemented.

The truth is that I had no problem unlocking Janis's phone. When I turned it on the welcome screen popped up. That was all I got. The phone had been restored to its factory settings. The micro-SD slot was empty.

I had a mental picture of someone going into Penn Station, sitting on one of the long, wooden benches, and resetting the phone. After they were done, they just left it there to be found. Maybe it would be picked up and carried off. Maybe it would be turned in. It didn't matter. It wasn't needed anymore.

Who was the "they?" One of her friends? Unlikely. The Brays? Then why call Alston? Uris? He was working a 1400-0200 tour that day. He could have done it. Murder her, leave the phone to start a false trail, then dump the luggage and her body, not necessarily in that order.

Or maybe it was Janis. Maybe she ran away from home. Kids do that, even ones as old as her. They do it for any number of reasons and sometimes for no reason at all. Being an adult, she had every right to do so. If she had run away, well, the question then was why.

Her laptop was different. Her browsing and download data had been deleted. That told me nothing. I do that myself on a regular basis. Everything else was there – shopping, entertainment, social media, even an eBook app.

I was going through her social media sites, not finding much beyond food, friends, selfies, and cute animals when Sergeant Richardson of Missing Persons called.

"There is no Jane Doe, sorry, unidentified female fitting Janis Bray's description in any hospital or morgue on this side of the Mississippi from Maine down to the Keys. Plus we called the ones on that list of friends you gave us, and then the other friends the first bunch told us about. Some of them knew she was going to New York but none of them were invited to go along. No luck with the ex-boyfriends either. And to finish with more negative results, nothing from the cab companies and all the rideshares want a subpoena."

"Thanks, Sarge, I'll be sure to mention your assistance to the Brays and you know who."

"Skip it, Grace. I don't think they care. I did it for you and the girl and not for them. Now can I get back to looking for lost kids?"

I told him he could and didn't even ask why his unit didn't check Penn Station's Lost and Found for Janis's phone.

That phone was the key, the phone and the one who left it. Another thing I wanted, maybe needed, was Janis's browsing history. I wanted to see what sites she had visited just before she supposedly left for New York.

I couldn't do anything about the first, I had subpoenaed Penn Station's security video and it wasn't in yet. As for the second … I called Webster.

Webster was a cyber wizard that I had used in the past when I needed computer skills that went beyond mine. He practiced mostly white magic with occasional trips to the grey side. He answered the phone with,

"What illegal crap are you going to ask me to do this time?"

"Hate to disappoint but this time it's legit. I'll email you the work order as soon as I hang up."

"Okay, but double the usual rate. The city just now sent the check from the last work I did for you."

I told him what I needed. He said no problem but it might take a day or two.

"Or maybe three, depending."

"On what?"

"How I feel."

If, as expected, the security video came the next day I may not need the browsing history. But it would show due diligence at trial, if there was one.

"Let's do this," I said and within minutes Webster had remote access to Janis's laptop and all its secrets.

The next day I was still waiting for the records from the rideshares but the Penn Station security video had come in. It clearly showed a person in a hooded jacket sit on the bench where Janis's phone was found. The suitcase this person was wheeling matched the description of the one missing from the set in Janis's closet. About ten minutes later the Amtrak for New York City was announced and the person wheeled their suitcase to the departure doors. The video from the platform showed my subject waiting for then getting on the northbound train.

Was my subject Janis, Uris, or someone else, maybe Nicholas Bray or a flunky? Janis could have been stealing from him, he found out, and well, Judge Copper did say he was a vindictive man.

The subject had taken great care not to face any cameras and I found myself wishing for TV software, the kind where you could zoom in on a blurry image and it suddenly becomes crystal clear. I'd then be able to read a clothing label and find out who bought it and where. The clerk would then conveniently remember seeing one or the other of my people of interest.

But all I had to work with was an eyeball estimate of the person's height based on what I saw on the videos. I finally decided that they were more likely to be a "he" than a "she" and went up to Mitchell Courthouse to get Judge Copper's signature.

One of the warrants was for Uris's phone. The other for his home, vehicle, any storage facilities he had rented, the patrol car he used, and his district locker. He was getting the full treatment, one that might hang him or move him down if not off the suspects' list.

Uris was not surprised or all that upset when he was called into his major's office. When I told him what was going down he just sighed, shrugged, and said, "I was wondering when this was coming. A rich daddy's girl is missing, probably presumed dead, and I'm the boyfriend. Plus the State's Attorney needs a badge in jail and I'm the best she's got. How we are doing this, Grace? Perp walk and news cameras?"

I shook my head. "As quietly as possible. The perp walk comes if you've been lying to me."

Uris opened his locker for my search. Nothing but a shower kit, a change of clothes, and a photo of Janis in a tight one-piece bathing suit on the inside locker door. His personal vehicle and his regular patrol car were "towed for repairs," cover for them being taken to the Crime Scene Unit's vehicle forensic bay.

"You know you're going to find …" Uris said when I told him about his cars.

"That depends, did you have protection?"

"I had my gun," he joked, then, "Didn't need it. We're both clean and she's on the Pill."

In the presence of his major, I recovered and signed for his service weapon, pepper spray, and baton. "You can get someone to drive you to the Quartermaster's to get replacements," I told him. "Just stay away from the processing bay."

I checked my watch. By now, my colleague Cole Williams was at Uris's home with two of the Crime Scene Unit's best technicians as they searched it for evidence of violence and murder.

Uris got his perp walk a few days later. Hair matted with blood was found in the trunk of his personal car. It was off to the side under a car charger. Hard to see without bright light, the CSI reported. Preliminary testing indicated that it most likely came from Janis. A 455nm blue light showed possible seminal fluid in the back seats of both his cars. Luminol highlighted traces of blood on the seats as well. Uris had already explained the former. As for the latter, he was done talking except to say that he didn't do it and that "we" were framing him – "we" being Alston, the Brays, and me.

Uris's phones and computers were clean. He had photos of Janis in bikinis and lingerie on both, but by today's standards they were PG-13. There was nothing to show he'd been thinking murder, planning murder, or looking for sites to dump a body. Not that he'd need to look any of that up. He was a well-trained cop, he'd been taught all that. His records showed that he had participated in a webinar on how to locate clandestine graves. Watched with a different mindset, the webinar also taught the viewer how to bury a body so that it would not be found.

The evidence was there but it was thin. If it had been a victim from a less than prominent family with a civilian suspect, I think Alston would have decided to wait for a body. But this was Baltimore, and Baltimore juries don't like or trust the police. Plus, Alston had a cop with a folder bulging with use of force reports and excessive force complaints. She had a missing girl and she had hair matted with the girl's blood. Not to mentioned sex in the back seat of a patrol car. *The Baltimore Truth* would put that bit of news on the front page.

Did I think he'd done it, killed her some reason and hid the body? It looked that way but something was bothering me. It bothered me when I wrote up my report and turned it in. It bothered me enough that I argued against the arrest and presentation to the Grand Jury. Argued the weakness of the case, argued for more time, argued that something seemed wrong even if I couldn't say what.

It was still bothering me when Alston called me into her office and, with the Brays in attendance, told me what a great job I had done. "Now all you need is a pike," she said just before Bray shook my hand in thanks and Ms. Bray hugged me a little too tightly.

My sources told me that Uris was offered a sweetheart deal – manslaughter, six years max at a minimum-security facility – if he gave up the body. He refused, saying that he didn't know where it was and didn't think she was dead.

I hadn't heard from Webster since I gave him remote access to Janis's laptop. He called back the day Uris's indictment was announced.

"Sorry," he said. "Someone who knows what they're doing, worse yet, knows what I do, set up this operating system. That's what happens when you can afford the best of the best. It took me some time to figure out how to find what you wanted."

"And did you?"

"Was Captain Jack Sparrow a real pirate?"

"No, he wasn't."

"Well then, it's a good thing I am."

Webster's own "Jolly Roger" appeared on my screen – a skull wearing a wizard's cap with two crossed wands beneath. It was followed by Janis's previously deleted browser and download history. As I looked at it – train schedules and routes, cities along those routes as far south as New Orleans and as far west as Seattle, bank accounts that were not listed as belonging to her – I realized what had been bothering me.

Webster had been waiting for me. When I got back to him he had changed his background to that of a tropical island, there was a pirate ship flying his flag offshore, and a dirt-eating smile on his face.

"Good job," I said. "Now find her for me."

"What?"

"You've got her whole life in front of you on that computer. Use her likes, dislikes, shopping history, whatever it takes, however long it takes. Find her."

"I don't know, Matthew, that's a pretty tall order. Not beyond my skills, of course, but expensive and time-consuming. Why don't we just try this?"

An address and phone number scrolled across the bottom of the screen. I wrote it down.

"How?"

He told me.

Not only does everyone lie (except God and Joshua Parker) but everyone makes mistakes. Even Parker. And yes, even SAO special investigators who think they know it all.

I told Sharon that I thought I knew where Janis's body was. Then I asked her not to tell Alston. "I'm not sure," I said. "Right now it's just a lead from a source. I need a couple of days to check it out and a couple of favors. And a train ticket."

A ten-hour train ride to Charlotte, NC. Then a three-hour drive to Wilmington. A stop, then another hour's drive to Holden Beach. Yeah, I could have flown but where's the fun in that. This way I got to ride a train.

Holden Beach is a nice area with retired couples in golf carts and lots of trees, lakes, and other areas suitable for hiding bodies. And there are gated communities suitable for hiding yourself.

I pulled into one such community, showing my badge to the

person guarding the gate, and followed the signs to the address a Wilmington pharmacist had given me, but only after she was served with subpoenae from the Baltimore SAO and the New Hanover County District Attorney's Office.

She looked like her photos, the ones her mother had given me. I will admit that the ones Uris had of her in bikinis and lingerie did flash into my mind but the married part of my brain made them go away.

"Janis Bray," I said, flashing my badge and calling her by her real name and not the one she'd used on her lease, "Matthew Grace, Baltimore City State's Attorney's Office. We've been looking for you."

Janis took the shock of being discovered fairly well. After a brief look of surprise, she invited me in, took me into the kitchen, and gave me a glass of sweet tea. (I think that's required by law anywhere south of Virginia.) She let me take a few sips before asking,

"How did you find me?"

"You did almost everything perfect. You should have taken your laptop with you, reformatted the drive, then dumped it somewhere. Or you should have searched for schedules, routes, and places to live on your phone. Mostly, you should have gone to the clinic down here to get your prescriptions rather than having them transferred to that Wilmington Pharmacy."

"I thought patient confidentiality would cover that."

I shook my head and took another sip of sweet tea. "Not when you're missing and presumed dead. He's been arrested."

Her first smile since she opened the door. "I know, it's been on the news. There's a TV station down here that runs stories about police all over the country who break the law. They call the segment, 'Bad Cop No Donut.' With him in jail, what made you keep looking for me?"

"Uris told me that he had been expecting to get served with a search warrant. He was a smart cop. If he had been guilty he would have bleached his patrol unit's back seat and had his personal car detailed. He would not have left anything for us to find."

I had some more sweet tea. When Janis realized my glass was half empty, she refilled it. She'd picked up Southern Hospitality very fast.

"You planned it well. The cell phone, wearing what I'm guessing was padding and an over-sized hoodie in the train station, just enough blood in the right places to get Uris arrested and maybe convicted."

"Probably convicted," she corrected.

I allowed that then asked, "Why?"

Janis's story started the same way as Uris's. Some favor for favor sex that grew into, well, not love but intense like. But then,

"He started trying to control me. Wanting to know where I was going and who with. Then he was telling me where to go."

"Just like your first father and your mother."

Her face darkened at this. She nodded and went on. "One night he picked me up in his police car. He parked somewhere dark and made me get in the back seat where he … used me."

"Did you want him to."

She shook her head. "He made it clear that I didn't have a choice. He did it once more in the police car and once in his own car. I should have done something, said something but I was afraid. Just like my mother was."

"What happened?" She was smart. She knew what I meant.

"It was about five weeks ago. He wanted me to go some stupid bull roast, 'to show me off,' he said. I told him that the last thing I wanted to do on a Saturday night was party with drunken cops. That's when he twisted my wrist and told me I didn't have a choice. I went, and by the time they were announcing the winners of the silent auction, I knew what I was going to do."

"Your second father, did he abuse you?"

"Not yet."

"So you framed Uris for your murder and stole Daddy's money." The bank accounts in her browser history.

She nodded. "He hides assets under my name and my mother's. One day I got some kind of document in the mail by mistake. From that, I figured out what he was doing. That night I went to his computer and withdrew some of 'my' money. He didn't say anything so I kept withdrawing. I have enough to live comfortably for the next few years and there's more when I need it."

Not for long, I thought, *just until Daddy figures it out.*

With her permission, I took her photo. Then I took a selfie of the two of us. Both were against a bare wall so as not to give anything away but they were enough to get Uris out of jail.

"Thank you, Ms. Bray. I'm done here." I moved to leave.

"What about me? What's going to happen?."

Janis had framed a man for a crime he didn't commit. That's her sin but I don't think it will bother her much. Whether she broke any laws, that wasn't up to me. Since I was in the South, I gave her the only answer I could.

"Frankly, Ms. Bray, I don't give a damn."

THE MARK OF CAIN

It was a few weeks after I found Janis Bray and got Officer Morgan Uris out of Central Booking when my wife and I both took some needed time off. We went to New York to celebrate my recent raise and promotion. Linda was the manager of the Baltimore Albion and was able to get us comped at its sister hotel in New York. No luck on the *Hamilton* tickets though we did get good seats at a great price for *The Book of Mormon* and *Smokey Joe's Cafe*.

We were having dinner in Frankie and Johnnies Steak House on 46th Street in Times Square when she asked, "So what happened to the girl?"

"What girl?"

"The one you found."

"Oh, that girl. I don't know. By the time her father sent his people to the address I gave him she was gone. I hope she does a better job hiding this time."

We then started talking about work, Linda telling stories about some of her hotel guests and me mostly complaining about Celina Alston, Baltimore's State's Attorney and the person who recently promoted me.

"Watch out for her, Matt. I don't think she likes you very much."

"She doesn't like me at all, which is fair, I don't like her. But most of the time Sharon acts as a buffer. Besides, I've dealt with worse."

"Like Jane Doe? You almost got killed on that case."

"Almost doesn't count."

Linda didn't agree so we talked about other things.

"Sharon and Sophie have asked us to be best couple at their wedding,' Linda mentioned casually.

"She didn't ask me, or even mention it."

"She didn't have to, did she? After all, she was a groomsperson at our wedding. By the way, I said yes for both of us."

"Good."

"Matt, you've told me how you two met, but never why she stopped being a defense attorney and joined the SAO."

I had asked her that myself over drinks when we celebrated my coming to work for her office as a forensic investigator. She gave me the short version, just enough to whet my interest. Being a naturally nosy induvial, I looked into it and got the rest of the story. So on the walk back to our hotel, I told it to Linda.

***

They met in a dark bar. The man who wanted murder done arrived first and took a seat in a booth near the back. The second man arrived shortly after. He got himself a drink, something soft. He was working that night, and he never mixed business with alcohol. He looked toward the back, then walked over to the man he knew to be his client. He sat across from him and lit a cigarette. The match flared up and briefly illuminated the client's face.

"You're Mr. Smith?" asked the man who had arrived first. He was nervous, constantly moving back and forth in his seat, glancing around to see if anyone was looking his way.

"As far as you're concerned I am." The man calling himself Smith spoke in a harsh whisper, his voice loud enough to be heard across the table but no further. "Tell me what you want, Barnes."

"You know what I want, that's why you're here."

"Say what you want or I walk."

"I'm not a cop, you don't have to worry about that, it's just that . . ."

Smith cut him off. "I know what you are. You were checked out. You're a contractor, you put up office buildings and apartments. Now say it."

"My wife, I want her dead. I want you to kill her."

"That wasn't so hard, was it?" Smith smiled, enjoying Barnes's discomfort. "You have something for me?"

Barnes took an envelope out of his inside topcoat pocket. "A picture of my wife, her personal information, her schedule."

"Anything else?"

A thicker envelope came out of the topcoat. Barnes handed it over. "Twenty thousand, like I was told." Smith picked up both envelopes and made them disappear. The bar was too dark for Barnes to tell where he had put them.

"When will you, you know, do it?"

Smith didn't answer right away. He finished his cigarette and lit another one. Again he used the light from the match to study his client. Pale complexion, black hair, slight scar at the right of the mouth forcing a half-smile. He'd know the man again.

"Best you don't know," Smith finally said. "That way you won't be stupid and go out of town or try to arrange an alibi. Cops pick up on that right away. Just keep to your regular schedule. You'll know when it happens."

"It will . . . will it look like an accident?"

"Or a mugging gone wrong, or a burglary, something like that." Smith wished he could see Barnes's face clearly without striking another match. Barnes was a weakling, a coward. He wasn't man enough to do the job himself, and now he was worried about how it was going to be done. Smith decided to twist the knife a little more.

"Lots of crime in this city, Barnes. The cops won't look too close at another street robbery, or rape."

Even in the darkness of the booth, Smith could see Barnes start at his last comment. He decided to leave him with that pleasant thought. He finished his soft drink and slid out of the booth.

"Wait for me to leave," he told Barnes. "In ten minutes, leave twenty on the table for the tab. Walk out without talking to anyone."

The man who called himself Smith left the bar. He did not stay around to see if Barnes did what he was told. He only hoped that the man would not do or say anything stupid when he talked to the cops. *Doesn't matter anyway*, Smith thought. *Even if he tells them all he knows, he doesn't know much. Not my name or where I'm from. I do the job clean, and the next day I'm out of Baltimore and heading home. Then I can take it easy until the next job. No problems.*

Smith wanted to wait a week but decided to move the job up a few days. He didn't want Barnes getting too edgy. He picked a night when Barnes was staying late for a company meeting. His wife went out, shopping probably. Smith went around to the rear of the house. There were woods in the back, no neighbors in view, and no outside lights. Breaking in was easy.

Once inside, he went up to the bedrooms, pulling out drawers and taking what cash he could find. Downstairs, he stacked the TV, DVD, and laptop next to the back door, taking care that none of what he did could be seen by anyone coming in through the front. Then he waited in the dark.

He sat by a window, behind a curtain, watching the street. If Barnes came home first, or if the wife brought a friend home, he'd be out the back door before they got to the front step.

Soon he saw a car pull up. Barnes's wife got out alone. She walked up with the key ready for the lock, just like all those rec center self-defense classes teach women to do. He stepped back, to be out of her view when she came in. He let her get inside and close the door.

He moved quickly. Before she knew he was there, he punched her once in the stomach, taking away her air. He covered her mouth and forced her against the door. Her back hit the doorknob. He pressed against her so she could not move. Then he put his hand to her throat and squeezed until he saw the life go out of her eyes.

Once she was dead, he let her fall. Bending over her body, he tore open her blouse just to give the cops something extra to think about. He dumped her purse, taking the cash out of her wallet. Finished with the job, he went out the way he came.

The other side of the woods met the back of a strip mall parking lot. His car was parked among dozens of others, in no way distinguishable. His dark clothing and the poor lighting on the lot insured that no one noticed him get into this car and drive away.

Back in his room, he made a bundle of the clothing he had worn on the job, stuffed it into a trash bag, and took it out to the motel's dumpster. It would be gone the next morning. On the way back, he stopped at the ice machine and filled a bucket. Back in his room, he poured himself a drink and sat back to watch some prime time TV, satisfied with a job well done.

They came for him three days later. Men armed with shotguns broke into his apartment late at night. The sledge hitting and shattering the door woke him up, but they were in his bedroom before he could react. Even if he were the type to keep a gun close at hand, it would not have done him any good. Before he could get out of bed, he was looking up at four very determined cops. Three of them wore ID jackets that said "FBI." The fourth cop wore a plain jacket but his baseball cap read "Baltimore Police." At least he knew why they were there.

With shotguns pointing, the cops let him put on some clothes. They read him his rights as he dressed. He'd heard them before. He wasn't going to talk to them and would call a lawyer as soon as the time was right. So he let them talk. He nodded in the right places and they were satisfied. As they lead him out, he idly wondered what mistake had led them to him.

Arrested by the FBI, he was in Federal custody until he got to Baltimore. Once there, papers were exchanged and he became the responsibility of the BPD. He was taken to the Central Booking Facility, charged with murder, and held without bail.

Detectives came to talk to him. They read him his rights again, then started asking him about the murder. He remained silent but didn't ask for a lawyer. With a lawyer, the questioning would end and he wanted to hear their questions. What they asked would tell him what they had, what their take on the crime was. When the one playing the good cop started talking about other burglaries in the neighborhood, he knew that it was something he did, a mistake he had made that put him in, that Barnes hadn't ratted him out. Knowing that, he finally asked to call an attorney.

Two days later, his lawyer came to the Fairfield Detention Center. He had been transferred there from Central Booking the day before. He was led into a small room, equipped only with a table and two chairs. He was loosely handcuffed to the chair farthest from the door, then his attorney was allowed to join him.

"Are they necessary?" the lawyer pointed to the cuffs. "Take them off right now," she told the officer who was about to leave.

"Sorry, Ma'am. The rules are that he stay cuffed." There were no such regulations and all three knew it. The attorney was about to protest when Smith stopped her.

"It's okay, it's loose enough." Smith held up his left hand. He took the bracelet in his right and moved it freely around his wrist. Then he lifted his arm to show the slack in the foot-long chain.

"It's not uncomfortable," he told the lawyer.

It was, though. It was another reminder of the extent to which he had lost control over his actions. The correctional officers saw him as having committed a real murder, taking down a taxpayer rather than killing someone in one of Baltimore's drug wars. For what he had done, for what they thought he had tried to do (*should never have ripped the blouse, John*), they made his life difficult at every chance.

So, it would do him no good to have his lawyer win a minor battle. It would only lead to more grief later.

The lawyer waited until the CO left then leaned over and offered her hand.

"John Ravenski, I'm Sharon Manchester. I'll be representing you."

Smith took her hand.

"Ms. Manchester, pleased to meet you, but call me Smith, at least in private."

"I'm not sure I understand, Mr. Ravenski . . . Smith."

"Not Mr. Smith, just Smith. That's who I am when I'm not at home. 'Ravenski' is a guy who lives in Philadelphia."

"But the police have arrested Ravenski, not Smith, so let's stick to that, and not give them any of your AKAs. "

Smith nodded his head in agreement. "Good idea. In that case, call me John."

"Fair enough, John, but I'm still Ms. Manchester."

Well, Smith thought, *that set the rules, didn't it*? He didn't mind, though. He had told his contact to get him the best criminal lawyer in Baltimore, and from all he had heard, there were only one or two others in this woman's league.

Manchester had opened her heavy briefcase and had taken out a file with his real name on it.

"What have they got on me?"

"They can put you on the scene, in the house the murder took place."

"Witnesses?" Smith figured that could have been the only way. One person had seen him coming out of the house, another saw him leaving the woods and getting into his car. Or maybe it was just one guy in the woods the whole time. No problem then, witnesses could be dealt with.

"No, no witnesses. The crime lab came up with physical evidence that says you were there."

"What kind of physical evidence?" Smith knew that he hadn't left any, none that could come back to him. That left him thinking frame. By why him? The cops would have done a local.

Manchester paged through her folder, looking for the lab reports.

"Here they are. There were fibers found near the back door where it had been forced. More were found at the victim's throat. So far, none have been matched to any of your clothing."

And none will, Smith's internal commentary continued, *since everything I wore I tossed. And I don't wear black in real life.*

"What else?" he asked aloud.

"The police traced you back to the motel. The lab searched and vacuumed the room, and the FBI did your Philadelphia apartment. Again, nothing."

"So what have they got?" Manchester had that look of saving the best for last. A good courtroom technique, but annoying right now.

"Not much, only the fingerprint match."

Smith's mind shut down. If she had told him that there had been a video camera that had recorded the whole murder he'd have been less surprised. "But I wore gloves the whole time," he wanted to shout at her, but he knew better than to admit guilt to anyone, even his lawyer.

The look on Manchester's face told him she had enjoyed her little surprise. *Just like I enjoyed playing with Barnes and the others*, Smith thought. He could tell that she did not like him, was probably sure of his guilt. She would still do her best for him, she seemed to be too good an attorney, but only her mind was in it, not her heart.

When he calmed down enough to talk, Smith asked, "Where were the prints found?"

Manchester picked up and read the lab report as if she didn't already know the answer. Reading from the report, she said, "The latent prints from the drinking glass found in the dish drainer on the kitchen counter have been identified as the right thumb and right forefinger of John Ravenski." She put down the report. "It was a computer match from the FBI files."

That interstate bust ten years ago, that's when I stopped being myself on jobs. Smith still could not figure out where the prints came from.

The lawyer put her reports away. "Really, John, no matter how thirsty you were, you should have waited until you were clear the scene to get a drink."

Suddenly it hit him. "That son of a bitch set me up." His fist hit the table, hard and loud enough that the CO looked in through the window in the door. Not seeing him attacking Manchester, he turned away again.

Manchester had, at first, been startled by his reaction. As Smith calmed down, she saw what might be a defense building. "Who set you up, John?"

Smith ignored her. He saw it all, meeting Barnes in the Pair o'Dice Lounge, making the deal, him leaving first. Then he pictured Barnes carefully picking up the glass he had been drinking from, putting it in the pocket of that big topcoat he was wearing. After finding the body, before calling the police, Barnes put it where the lab would find it.

But why? Barnes had already paid. Guilt maybe, or payback for the rape threat. If he thought that Smith would stay quiet, that was a bigger mistake than Smith leaving the glass behind. *If I go down, he goes with me*, Smith promised himself. Barnes had to know that if Smith were arrested, he would be too. Still, it was his word against Barnes, and no proof other than his word. Any accusation would look like a last-ditch effort.

"John. Mr. Ravenski. Smith!" Shouting his chosen name, Manchester finally got through to Smith. He came out of his reverie.

"Ms. Manchester," he said without excusing his fugue, "what's the police take on the killing?"

"They see it as a B&E. There had been a few in the neighborhood. They figure you had come down to do the crimes. This one went bad and you decided to get the hell out of Dodge. And except for that one mistake with the drink, you'd have gotten away with all of them."

Manchester let him take that in, then asked, "Now what's this about getting set up?"

Smith ignored her. He thought for a moment, then asked her, "They talking death penalty?"

Manchester nodded. "A murder committed during another felony with evidence of an attempted sexual assault. Add to that the political situation. Too many minorities on the Row. The State's Attorney's been waiting for an eligible white male to balance the population. You're it."

That decided him. "Tell them I want to deal."

Manchester dismissed that with a wave. "You don't have anything to deal with, John. They got you inside the house, with no previous relationship with either the victim or her husband."

"Well, Ms. Manchester, that's not exactly true."

Smith laid it out for her. He told her about meeting Barnes in the Pair o' Dice, about Barnes hiring him to do the murder, and why the BPD or FBI would not be making any fiber matches. He then told her of his theory on how his prints got on the drinking glass.

"You know how that sounds, don't you?"

"Yeah, like I'm desperate and grabbing at straws. But consider this. The glass my prints were on, it won't match any other glass in the Barnes home. However, it should have about fifty twins in the

Pair o'Dice. The bartender there should be able to put Barnes and me together. If need be, I'll take a polygraph and pick Barnes out of a line-up." Smith let out a short, bitter laugh. "Hell, work it right, Ms. Manchester, and you can present me as the innocent victim of an elaborate frame."

Manchester considered this for a moment, then shook her head. "It won't be enough, John. The police aren't stupid. They'll know it for what it was, conspiracy to commit murder. They won't see you as an innocent victim."

"They won't, but a jury might, and the State's Attorney will realize that. Give him a choice. He can have both me and Barnes, or he can take the chance on losing us both."

"He might go for that, he might not. Is there anything else you can give me?"

"Write this down." Smith gave her three names. "These guys were mobbed up. The first in Chicago, the second in Cleveland, the last in Boston. All three were turned by the Feds. None of them made it to trial."

"You killed them?"

"For now, let's just say that I can point the way to the ones who gave the orders, and supply proof as needed. I'll give the Feds these three and the BPD can have Barnes, all part of the same deal."

Suddenly dealing with much more than a simple murder, Manchester took some time to think. Smith just sat back and watched her work through the possibilities.

"John, if what you're telling me is true, then giving up the details of the other three murders would establish your, well, I don't want to use the word credibility . . ."

"Try credentials."

"Your credentials, then, as a hitman. The Baltimore State's Attorney would then probably accept some kind of plea for your testimony against Barnes. My question to you is, what are you willing to take?"

"Make the best deal you can, no more than twenty."

"That's a long time."

"I won't serve it. The FBI, the DEA, a few others will claim me. I'll do Federal time. After some jobs, I'll be out in five."

"What do you mean, 'some jobs'?"

"Lawyer/client privilege?"

Manchester nodded, "Of course."

"Ms. Manchester, imagine an inmate serving multiple life with no chance of parole. Now, this man kills another inmate or, worse yet, a guard. Besides the death penalty, which takes too long and costs too much, what can they do? What can happen to this man?"

"I have no idea."

"Oh yes, you do. I can tell from the look in your eyes that you've figured it out. I happen to him, or someone just like me. When a prison has a con they can't control, one who has nothing left to lose, well, the Feds send someone like me in. He gets taken out and order is restored. Each job counts as so many years served. They call it 'cooperation in other matters'."

Manchester was quiet. Smith knew he had laid a heavy burden on her, one she could talk about only to others covered by their privilege. She gathered up her papers and began to leave.

"I'll do what I can, John. No promises, but I should be able to make some kind of deal."

"I'll be waiting to hear from you."

Smith did not have to wait long. Within three days, he and Manchester were back in the interview room.

"The Feds almost beat me to the State's Attorney," she told him. "It took them a while, but they finally connected John Ravenski to the Smith they've been tracking for the last three years."

"They're slow but not stupid. What happened?"

"The FBI called just as I was pitching the deal to the ASA. You can forget the line-up and the polygraph. The bartender at the Pair o'Dice picked Barnes out of a photo six-pack. He remembers seeing the two of you together. And the glasses match."

"So what are they offering?"

"Here's the best I could do. You take a plea on the murder, testify against Barnes; you'll get ten to twenty. After the trial, you'll be transferred to Federal custody. Once there, you tell them what you can about the other three killings. Given your full cooperation with this and 'other matters,' you can expect a significant sentence reduction."

"Where do I sign?"

Leonard Barnes was arrested the next day. His trial was well attended. The media was more than well-represented, the story of murder for hire being the lead item on all four of the local news broadcasts. Except for his brother, who had to take care of the family contracting business, Barnes's entire family was there. They were usually quoted on the evening news as being sure that Leonard had no part in this sordid business. The family of Lois Barnes, the deceased, was also present. In their turn, they had always been sure that Leonard would come to a bad end, although they never suspected that he was capable of murder. At least, that's what they told the TV cameras.

Maryland law did not permit cameras in the courtroom, so the day Smith testified was the first time he saw Barnes since that night in the Pair o'Dice Lounge.

He looked smaller from the witness stand, and paler. *I guess being arrested for murder will do that to some people*, Smith thought. He still wondered why Barnes had set him up. Smith gave his testimony in a flat, toneless voice, letting the jury read whatever they wanted into his lack of expression.

The defense tried to make an issue of his plea bargain, but Smith could tell that to most of the jurors, twenty years did not seem like much of a deal. His arrangement with the Feds was not mentioned by either side.

As he finished his testimony, Smith again looked over at Barnes. The man had kept his head down most of the time, but as Smith left the stand, he picked up his head and looked right at him. The expression on his face was one of bewilderment, as if asking how Smith could have said the things he did. The smile Smith remembered from the bar was gone. *Wiped it right off his face I did*, he said to himself.

It wasn't until he was back in his jail cell when he realized what Barnes's lack of a smile meant.

Frank Barnes got to work early. Ever since Leonard had been

arrested, he'd had to do both his and his brother's share of the work. That meant coming in before dawn and staying late into the evening. Frank didn't mind. It would be worth it once he had the business organized the way he liked it. Then he could sit back and relax. The deals he would make with the unions and the men behind them would see to that. He'd do less work and make more money, money he would not have to share with Leonard. His brother had high legal fees. He'd already offered to sell his share of the business to Frank. The price Frank offered him was low, but Leonard believed Frank when he told him that it was the best he could do. Needing the money, Leonard was in no position to bargain.

Frank had been working for an hour when the trailer door opened and Smith walked in. Without waiting for an invitation, Smith sat down in front of Frank's desk.

"Morning, Barnes, remember me?"

Frank said nothing. In the light coming from the window, the scar on the right side of his mouth was more visible than it had been in the bar, the half-smile more noticeable. Except for the scar, he was a good match for his brother. Smith saw Frank's arm drop as he started to reach for something in a lower desk drawer.

"If that's a gun, remember what I do for a living, and don't be foolish."

Frank's arm straightened and came from behind the desk. "How did you get out?"

"I've got friends, Barnes, or rather, the people I work for do. As soon as I realized that Leonard hadn't set me up, I called some of them. Arrangements were made. There was a 'mix-up' at the Detention Center, and some of the wrong people were 'accidentally' released. As soon as I was out, I came to see you."

Despite the coolness of the trailer, Frank was starting to sweat. "I don't know what you mean. I've never seen you before."

Smith's voice took on a menacing tone. "Don't play games, Barnes. You set me up. It was your brother's house. You planted that glass for the police to find. And if they hadn't, I'm sure you would have tipped them off some other way."

"What do you want?"

"What I want, Barnes, is to do you like I did your sister-in-law, but that wouldn't help me any. The way I see it, I helped you get rid of your brother as well as his wife. That makes another twenty you owe me." Smith looked toward the safe behind Frank's desk. Frank caught the look.

"I've got fifteen in the safe, the week's payroll. I can give you that, and the other five when I go to the bank to replace it."

Smith pretended to think it over. Finally, he said, "I'll settle for the fifteen and an explanation. Why use me to set up your brother, why not just have me take him out?"

Frank's explanation was reluctant and halting. He didn't want to give it, but he was afraid of what the man in front of him would do if he refused.

"I wanted the business. If Leonard were killed, his share of it would have gone to Lois. I could have bought her out, but she might have wanted to look at the books, and I couldn't afford that. Leonard and I look enough alike. Most people mistake us for each other."

"Except for the scar."

"Yeah, except for the scar." Frank reached up and ran his hand along the right side of his mouth.

"I figured if I had his wife killed, then made it look like Leonard had arranged it, he'd be forced to sell his share of the business to me to pay his legal fees. I thought the bar was dark enough so you wouldn't notice the scar. That's why I stayed away from the trial.

"At first I was just going to phone in a tip to the cops – who you were, how they could get in touch with your contacts. Then when you left the bar and I saw that glass on the table, I got the idea to leave it in Leonard's house. If you did her in the house before anyone noticed the glass, they'd find your prints. If not, no harm done."

Smith stayed quiet long enough to make Frank afraid that he was going to forget about the fifteen thousand and take personal vengeance. Smith was thinking about it, and under other circumstances would have after getting the money. Instead, he just nodded slightly, as if accepting what he'd been told.

"Get the money."

Frank turned around, opened and emptied the safe. He stood back to show Smith that there was nothing left inside but papers. He took a manila envelope off his desk and put the cash inside. He handed it over. Smith took the money, stood up, and turned to go.

"This makes us even, right?" Frank asked him when he was almost at the door.

"Almost." Smith left, leaving Frank to worry about what he meant.

Smith had not gone more than five feet off the site when two detectives, one local, one FBI, came up to him. He knew there were more nearby. He handed over the money and held his hands out for the cuffs.

"You get it all?" he asked the Fed.

"Clear as a bell," the detective answered. He reached into Smith's coat and took out the microphone.

Smith turned toward the site and watched as the police broke into the trailer to arrest Frank Barnes. *There'll be another trial*, he thought, *then five years or so of prison, doing the system's dirty jobs. After that, well, I'll be out, but it won't be the same. Can't go back to freelance*. He looked over at the Fed designated as his keeper. *It will be work for them or not at all, or else get an honest job.*

Smith again turned his attention to the trailer. They brought Frank Barnes out in handcuffs. Smith had wanted to be put in the same wagon as Barnes for transport, but the cops weren't being that accommodating.

Smith watched the man who had cost him five years of his life being taken away. To himself, he said the words that he'd make sure Barnes would soon hear.

"There's a mark on you, Barnes. Like I said, we're almost even. I'll see you again, or a friend of mine will, and you'll serve your time, the rest of your life, in pain. Then we'll be even."

Smith's ride came. He was put into the back of a caged police car and taken off to begin his own long journey.

***

We were almost at the hotel when I finished the story.

"Soon after that, Sharon decided that she didn't want to work for people like Ravenski anymore."

"How do you know all this?" Linda wanted to know.

"I talked to a guy who talked to a guy who had 'business dealings' with Ravenski. Funny, thing, the second guy called himself 'Smith' as well."

When we got to our room, the curtains were opened to a nighttime view of New York. Then we forgot all about my job, her job, hitmen, and the view, and just thought about each other.

COLLATERAL DAMAGE

It was the third sunny day in a row, just the right time to cut the grass, or so Tyrone Grant's wife told him.

"I can take a hint," he said, grudgingly turning off whatever mystery Jessica Fletcher was trying to solve on the Hallmark channel.

"You couldn't last night," she called back to him but by then he was heading down to the basement. Changing into his outdoor clothes, he got out his old Sears Kenmore electric mower and wheeled it into his back yard.

Before he got started, he took a look at his grass. Over the years he had put a lot of work into his lawn and the work showed. It had survived two kids, three dogs, and the birdseed incident when Roberta had put up feeders that spilled over into the grass. Soon all sorts of things were growing. It had taken the rest of the summer and part of the following spring before things looked good again. The feeder was moved to the back porch until the squirrels showed up. After that, Roberta settled for a birdbath in the middle of her garden.

As usual, Tyrone looked left then right, comparing the green on the other sides of the fences to his. Satisfied that he wasn't letting the neighborhood down, he pressed the start button, pulled back the safety bar, and went to work.

He finished the back and decided to do all the mowing before he started the edging. After doing both sides he started on the front. He was just thinking that his wife had been right, that it was a good day to cut the grass, when the bullet hit him.

The first one had missed, striking and cracking the concrete of Tyrone's front porch. Despite being electric, his old mover was noisy so he did not hear the sound of the shot or the impact of the bullet hitting the porch.

He didn't hear the second shot either, the one that smashed into his chest when he turned to start another row. As the bullet went through him, Tyrone's last thought was *Heart attack* as he clutched his chest and fell to the ground, the mower stopping automatically when he lost his grip on the safety bar.

Others had heard the shots. This being Baltimore, where the sounds of gunfire were not uncommon, they knew them for what they were. And when they saw Tyrone go down, they knew what had happened and called it in. Some of the callers actually waited for the police to arrive, to bear witness to a man's last few minutes on Earth.

Soon the block of Glenmore Avenue where Tyrone Grant had lived was roped off by yellow and black crime scene tape, as was the park across the street from Tyrone's house. Uniformed officers canvassed the neighborhood. Detectives took statements from witnesses as to when and where they were when they heard the shots. Crime Scene Investigators took photographs, drew diagrams, and used metal detectors to search the area of lawn where, judging from the positions of the mower and Tyrone's body, the second bullet had to have buried itself.

The few witnesses who had come forward all agreed on the time of the shooting and that the shots seemed to have come from the park. None of them saw anything – no one running from the park, no one carrying a rifle-shaped object, no car speeding away.

Cadets from the current police academy class arrived by bus to search the park for cartridge cases and other evidence.

"Think they'll find anything, Travis?" Detective Abel Jook asked the crime scene tech who had come over to report that the second bullet had been found.

"They might. At least we have the bullet."

"Is it in good shape?"

"Better than the first one."

The search from the east side of the park to the west took over an hour. When it was over, the cartridge cases had not been found. So Homicide Lieutenant Joshua Parker had the academy class search the park from north to south. This time, a sharp-eyed cadet caught a gleam of shiny brass and reached down to claim her prize.

"DO NOT TOUCH THAT!" Parker's roar froze the cadet in her place. Then, with the integrity of the evidence now safe, he said in a calmer voice, "Somebody get the Crime Lab down here. Tell them I want the sketch expanded and a measurement of how far the casings were from the body."

Crime scene people, officers, and detectives worked into the evening. Finally, the scene was secured and the street and the park were given back to the neighborhood.

There were reports to be written and evidence to be submitted. Once that was done, the hard work would begin, that of finding out who killed Tyrone Grant and why.

The Firearms Unit reported that the two cartridge cases were .308 Winchesters and had been fired from the same weapon. The bullets were consistent with that caliber. Neither the bullets nor the casings matched anything in the Integrated Ballistics Identification System. No latent prints or DNA were found on the cartridge cases. Detectives determined that Tyrone Grant had no adult or juvenile criminal record, did not use or abuse legal or illegal drugs, did not have any questionable material on his computer or suspicious texts on his phone, and was not in any financial difficulty. Interviews with friends, family, and coworkers all indicated that he was well liked by all.

"So we have nothing," Lieutenant Parker asked during the weekly review of open cases.

"Nothing," Detective Jook reluctantly agreed. "We could find no reason why he should have been killed." Jook looked around as if to spread the blame for Tyrone Grant's name still being in red on the murder board. "We figure it was either a stray shot, someone shooting at someone else and missing, or mistaken identity. We may never know unless …"

Jook did not have to finish his thought. Every man and woman around the conference table knew what followed "unless …"

Unless someone else is shot or killed by the same weapon.

"Let us pray that doesn't happen," Lieutenant Parker said.

It has been said that homicide detectives work for God. That may be true in most cities but in the Baltimore Police Department it is believed that its detectives work for Joshua Parker, who is God's appointed representative to the BPD. This may or may not be so, but if it is, then this was one of those times that the Almighty chose not to answer the prayer of Their servant.

The call came in a little after eight in the morning, a man killed outside Lucky Dan's convenience store on Park Heights Avenue. Detective Don Morris took the call, thinking that this was just another Baltimore street shooting. *Maybe this time there'll be some usable evidence*, he silently wished. M*aybe this time a witness will step up and say who did it. Maybe this time a street or business camera will catch the whole thing going down.*

And maybe one day Buzz McHale will retire and the mayor will appoint me commissioner, Don thought as he pulled up on an all too familiar scene.

A crowd of people stood around the yellow tape – some curious, some waiting for the tape to come down so they could get into the store. Ducking under the tape, Don found the primary officer and asked, "What have we got?"

"We got some witnesses who said the dead guy," the officer pointed to the blanket-covered form just outside a shattered glass door, "was just standing there when there was a shot and he went down."

"Did our witnesses say who did it?"

"They all said, and there were seven of them, that there was nobody near him when he was shot."

"And we believe them?"

The uniformed officer nodded. "This time, yeah. The surveillance cameras caught it all. Go check it out."

Don looked at the door, saw that the top half of its glass was still hanging precariously in place, and decided to go around the back way.

The videos showed it clearly. One camera showed the victim, Ronald Thayer, about to enter the store. Then he was on the ground, the bottom part of the door exploding into glass fragments. Two other cameras gave Don a 180° ground-level view of the parking lot as well as Park Heights Avenue. There was the usual traffic, people walking back and forth, but nobody who looked like he was pointing a gun anywhere near Thayer.

For a moment, the detective just stood there, looking at the door, its glass, the body. He looked across the street. Then he squatted down and looked again. He called to the primary through the door.

"Did you see the body?"

"Yes, sir."

"Where were the wounds?"

"Upper back, out the lower front."

Downward angle. From his crouched position Don looked at the houses across the street. "Tell your sergeant that we're going to need all the vacant houses across the street secured. I'll call in for warrants."

Don stood up slowly, hearing and feeling joints creak that hadn't creaked five years ago. As he turned, he saw the CSI come in. She was carrying a broom she had taken from the back of the store.

"Got all your photos, Jennifer?" he asked.

She smiled. "Except for the sketch I was done before you got here. I'm going to sweep this mess up and see if I can find the ..."

Just then there was a loud crash. Both detective and CSI jumped as gravity claimed the glass remaining in the door. When the last piece had fallen Jennifer just shrugged and said, "More to sweep up."

Don left her to her job saying, "Wear your heavy-duty gloves."

"Always."

Don had been on the phone for five minutes discussing with Parker the need for multiple search warrants versus one warrant to cover the entire block. It was then that Jennifer came up to him and showed him the bullet she had found in the glass.

It was not the usual 9mm or .380. It was instead a rifle bullet and something told the detective that it would be a match for the one that had killed Tyrone Grant.

After a quick explanation, the lieutenant said, "You'll have your warrants." Parker then called Commissioner McHale, who called the mayor, who called the State's Attorney's Office. Thirty minutes later, Judge Gertrude Deveraux was signing warrants for the vacant houses only. "Tell your officers to use their charm to get into the occupied ones."

Charm was not needed. A .308 Winchester cartridge case was found in the house directly across from Lucky Dan's. It was on the floor of the front bedroom just near the window.

Don sighed. "Get another CSU team in here. Tell them to dust everything." He looked out the window, taking in the sniper's view – the store, the broken door, the sheet-covered body. A media storm was coming, and he was going to be in the middle of it.

I should have gone out for coffee and let the damned phone ring, he thought.

Once the news broke, the media went crazy, comparing the present murders to the Beltway Sniper shootings of October 2002. *The Baltimore Truth* ran an article speculating that there may have been a third shooter along with the two men who had been convicted in that case. This was a reasoned argument compared to the theories which erupted overnight on the Internet and social media which put the blame on everything from the extremes of the right and left wings to a secret cadre of funeral home directors and florists out to create business.

"No links between Grant and Thayer," Detective Jook reported in the Homicide Unit's weekly briefing, which was now being held daily. "Other than they were both killed by the same weapon."

"Lots of prints from the house," Don Morris reported. "Mostly from the bottles and food containers left behind by the countless homeless people who use the vacants for shelter. The Latent Print Unit is running the lifts though AFIS now. Probably get hits on some burglaries."

"Maybe we'll get lucky and hit on someone who saw a guy with a rifle," Jook offered.

"Good call on getting the warrants, Detective Morris," Joshua Parker said. "If anyone was using the vacants as their home and something comes from the prints, they can't claim their rights were violated. Now, where do we go from here?"

As the lieutenant listened to the comments and opinions from the primary detectives involved as well as the other investigators in the room, he thought it possible that one of the homeless people who frequented the vacant houses may have seen something, if not the morning of the shooting then before that, someone casing the houses, looking for the best angle from which to shoot someone.

Thoughts of doing a homeless sweep in Northwest Baltimore passed through Parker's mind and were immediately rejected. *Best get the advocates for the homeless involved*, he decided. Better still, team one of his detectives with one of the advocates. He made a note to do that, just as soon he checked to see who had the lowest clearance rate.

There was nothing else to do except try to find a link between the victims and pray that rumors would not overwhelm common sense and set Baltimore afire – again.

This time Parker's prayers were answered. The city stayed calm, people were worried but not scared. A week went by with no further sniper-style shootings. Then another week. The sniper task force was reduced to just Detectives Jook and Morris.

It was the third week when things almost blew up. Reverend Jerome Fells, a minister of a small Eastside church, was outside saying farewell to his congregation as they left his Sunday morning services. There was a crack. As the reverend fell dead to the ground, his blood spattered the three women to whom he was speaking.

One of the women collapsed, the second screamed and ran away. The third, a nurse, bent over the fallen man to render aid, only to find that he had gone to God. After a quick prayer, she turned her attention to the woman who had fallen and began CPR.

Witnesses reported seeing a back van drive away. No one got a tag number.

THE SNIPER RETURNS was the headline of the next day's *Baltimore Sun*.

HE'S BACK – WHO WILL BE NEXT was the banner of *The Baltimore Truth*.

Given that all three of the victims had been black, it was inevitable that both papers, all four TV stations, and every other media outlet questioned whether these shootings presaged the beginning of a war against Baltimore's African-American Community.

The specter of Ollie Wallace again reared its head. Wallace was a drug dealer and burglar who had died under suspicious circumstances while in the custody of the police. His death was followed by protests and demonstrations which paralyzed the city and led to riots, lootings, and deaths. More demonstrations, another riot, and more deaths occurred when the five officers involved in Wallace's death were acquitted in a bench trial.

But before any protests could be staged, before any massive demonstrations could again shut down a square mile of traffic, before any damage could be done, the city was ironically saved by the sniper.

Jerald Fry was working in his Patapsco Avenue law office. He had just reviewed his list of clients and was looking across to the Hargrove District Courthouse when a .308 bullet shattered his window and killed him at his desk. His body was not found until his secretary came in thirty minutes later.

Fry had been white. He had also been shot with the same rifle that had killed the other three. Worries about someone targeting blacks waned as fears of a random sniper grew. Games were canceled, outdoor school events were postponed, and tourism in Baltimore dropped off. Police found excuses to stop black vans.

"So what's Parker thinking these days?" I asked Detective Jook when he stopped at my office to drop off reports on what the media was now calling "The Winchester Sniper." In my new position as Special Investigator for the State's Attorney's Office, it was part of my job to monitor the police investigation into the sniper shootings. Monitor – not supervise, criticize, or even participate.

"Tell Her that the SAO doesn't get involved until an arrest is made," Parker said when I asked him to forward copies of his reports. "Her" was Celina Alston, State's Attorney for Baltimore City. Police hate her so much that few below the rank of Major will refer to her by name. That's because she keeps trying to put them in jail whether they deserve it or not. Her new policy is that every police-involved shooting or serious use of force gets presented to the Grand Jury. No indictments yet but it's only a matter of time. She also wanted to replace the BPD's Internal Affairs Division with independent, outside investigators. To be honest, I couldn't find fault with either proposal.

Detective Jook was small and slender with thinning gray hair. A Japanese great-grandmother with strong genes was responsible for his slight Asian features, which seemed at odds with his dark skin and Boston accent. Overall, he didn't look like a detective, a fact which helped more than hindered him. Most witnesses and suspects were so busy trying to figure out just what he was that they didn't realize he was leading them down the road to a statement or confession.

"With all that's going on, he's thinking about retiring, Grace," Jook said with a smile.

"Parker will never retire. Come the end times Parker will still be standing, ready to lead the investigation into who caused the Apocalypse." *And those of us who know him will probably be standing with him, waiting for his orders*, I thought but didn't say. "Besides, if he ever does pack it in, he'll want to go out on a win. Has he thought of the 'kill four to hide one' theory yet?"

Jook nodded. "He's got four detectives each looking at one of the victims to see who might want them dead. Plus he's got people looking for any connection among the four."

"Join the club," I said, pointing to my computer.

Jook nodded then excused himself with, "Crime doesn't solve itself, and there are too many names in red and not enough in black on the murder board."

Other than reviewing the BPD's progress, or lack thereof, with the investigation, one of the sniper-related jobs Alston had given me was to play the game everyone in Baltimore was playing. What linked the four victims?

It was Murphy of *The Baltimore Truth* who won the game. I wish I could say that I was a close second but I was nowhere near the finish line. *The Truth* broke the story in a rare special edition. All four men – Tyrone Grant, Ronald Thayer, Reverend Jerome

Fells, and Jerald Fry had been among those tens of thousands of people who had marched in protest over the death of Ollie Wallace and again when the officers accused of that death were acquitted.

Murphy had suspected the connection after a marathon review of Reverend Fells's Facebook page. There he found photos of Fells marching east on a crowd-filled Pratt Street, with the cars behind the protestors backed up for at least a mile with no place to go and no way to leave. That photo was from the first set of demonstrations. During the second most drivers had the sense to avoid downtown from Federal Hill up to and beyond City Hall.

If this were a TV show, the photos would have shown Grant, Thayer, and Fry marching arm-in-arm with the reverend. But it's only that easy on TV. Instead, Murphy dug deep in the online history of the protests and the other three men and managed to find photos of their involvement as well.

Murphy didn't go any further than that. He had found the connection, he had found his headline, and now he had a story that *The Baltimore Truth* could run with for weeks.

WHO'S NEXT? Ran the banner headline of *The Truth's* special edition. Below that, in slightly a slightly smaller font size, was the warning IF YOU MARCHED YOU ARE A TARGET.

I wish I could tell you that the city stayed calm. I wish I could tell you that the police were not deluged with demands for protection. I wish I could tell that the Governor did not consider calling out the National Guard and putting Baltimore under martial law. I wish I could tell you that lawyers did not run ads on local TV urging those who had marched to sue the City of Baltimore for putting their lives in danger. And I wish I could tell you that a large number of people did not think that the police had somehow obtained the names of all the protestors and, for some reason, was now hunting them down one by one.

I wish I could tell you this, but I can't.

"You know what's next, Matthew," Sharon Manchester, my immediate supervisor, asked me the day after *The Baltimore Truth* broke the story.

I did. "Alston's going to go crazy." Not hearing any disagreement

I went on. "She'll convene a Grand Jury. She'll demand an outside investigation and she'll get it. The Feds have been itching to get involved in this ever since Thayer went down. This will be their chance. With all the stories about BPD involvement going around, every cop will be a suspect and if, no, when the next body falls it will be Ollie Wallace all over again."

This was a worst-case scenario but at the time it seemed all too possible.

Just then Sharon's phone rang. After she answered it I heard her say. "Yes, I'm here with him now. Yes, I'll tell him. Goodbye, Celina."

"Does she want to see me?"

Sharon shook her head. "She told me to tell her special investigator to solve this case before anyone else does, preferably before there's a fifth victim."

My first thought after Sharon walked away was that I should have taken the hotel job my wife kept offering me. My next was that I should have put in for two weeks' vacation as soon as *The Truth* broke the story. Then I started thinking about the guy behind the rifle. The guy who put four people in his sights and pulled the trigger. The guy who right now might be searching the Internet for photos of the Ollie Wallace demonstrations and matching faces to names and names to addresses to find his next targets. The guy who was now my target.

I felt that small tingle of excitement I sometimes got back when I was a crime scene technician and later as a private investigator. I was again playing the game of cops and robbers, this time against someone who was terrorizing the city.

I tried to forget that the last time I had played for such high stakes I'd almost been killed. Instead, I went back six years to the riots and demonstrations and tried to think of a reason someone would want to kill those involved.

Ruling out most of the deadly sins I found myself left with Greed and Anger. Maybe it was "kill four to hide one" and there was insurance money or inheritance involved. If so, Parker and his crew would find that out. It was too involved to be another "Riot for Profit" scheme. It was quicker and easier to shoot a couple of people then scream loud and long that the police did it. No, I couldn't see a money motive in this.

That left me with Anger, or maybe Anger's cousin Vengeance. Vengeance might belong to the Lord but it has long been practiced by Baltimore gangs. In Baltimore, there's no such thing as a single gang shooting. The first shooting prompts a payback hit which has to be answered and so forth. But any such revenge for a death that occurred during the riots would have happened then and not six years later. Which also rules out retaliation by police officers for injuries received. They too would have acted swiftly and against those directly involved.

I found myself looking at those killed during the Wallace disturbances. There were six, four from right after Wallace died and two after the officers' acquittals.

Two of the six were shot by shopkeepers whose stores were being looted. No charges, no payback. One was killed by a rock thrown at police which fell short and hit one of the demonstrators in the head. An argument over the spoils from a drugstore left one dead on the scene and another later dying in the hospital. Gravity killed one woman. She was climbing through a broken front display window when a shard of glass fell and cut her carotid artery. She bled to death before the ambulance could get to her. According to the report on that one, even if the paramedics had not been held up by the crowd, there would have been nothing for them to do but pronounce her dead.

There were also three deaths included in the final report that were ruled the result of medical causes. These were not considered riot-related but were included as "incidental deaths."

It is said that revenge is a dish best served cold but six years is a long time to keep something in a freezer. None of the sniper's victims were involved in any way with the six deaths. And there was nothing in the record of those deaths that would have prompted long-delayed revenge.

I was bothered by the phrase "incidental deaths," as if one person's death were less important than another's.

Two heart attacks and a stroke. The stroke and one of the heart attacks occurred in the streets where the demonstrations were taking place. Even if there had been a doctor standing right by them, there was nothing that could have been done for either victim. Earle Slater (heart attack) was pronounced dead on the scene. Kendrick Riddle (stroke) died a month later in the hospital in the presence of his family.

As for the other heart attack victim, to my mind there was nothing "incidental" about it. Six years ago, Edward Lochner and his wife Sonya were out driving when she started having chest pains. Rather than wait for an ambulance, Lochner decided to drive his wife to the hospital. It was, after all, only ten minutes away. Except that they ran into the first of the Ollie Wallace demonstrations.

They became stuck, unable to go back, unable to move forward. Lochner called 911 but ambulances could not get to them. A Medic-Vac copter was dispatched but arrived too late. Sonya Lochner was DOA in her car.

It was late and I was tired. It was time to leave, time to go home to Linda. But I didn't. I didn't want to go home and tell my wife that I was about to do something dangerous, again. And the sniper worked mornings. If he struck tomorrow and I could have stopped him, the death would be on my hands, and that sort of blood never washes off.

I called Linda and told her that I had to work late. I told her that I loved her. She said that she loved me too. She told me to come home as soon as I could, that she'd have something hot waiting for me. And that she'd have dinner waiting as well.

That made me not want to make my next call. But with a sigh, I called Detective Jook.

"Why not call Parker?" he asked when I told him what I wanted.

"It's a not a Parker kind jof case."

Parker would want to do things by the book. That would mean SWAT and a probable barricade situation. Flashbangs. Gunfire maybe, people getting shot or killed. Four deaths were enough.

"There are others I could ask but it's your case. I thought you'd want to be in on it."

Jook didn't hesitate. "Where and when."

"Glenmore and Hilltop. As soon as possible."

My position as an SAO special investigator came with a badge and the right to carry a weapon. I thought about the .38 revolver I kept in a lockbox bolted to the bottom left drawer of my desk. It had been given to me by a PI friend from Brooklyn when I first went into private practice. Except at the range, I had never fired it. Thinking of all the ways things could go wrong, I almost strapped it on. Instead, I left without it. Four deaths were enough.

Lochner lived on Mayberry just off of Walther. His house was a two-minute walk to the park from where the sniper had shot Tyrone Grant. We parked our cars on Walther and walked two houses down on Mayberry to Lochner's house. His downstairs lights were on.

"Do you have the warrant?" Jook asked.

"What warrant?" I asked. Warrants ring bells, bells I didn't want rung. "I told you this wasn't a Parker kind of case. Besides, we're just going to talk, not search and seize. That can come later."

When I knocked on the door I noticed that Jook's hand was inside his jacket, just in case Lochner came to the door with his rifle.

An unarmed Lochner opened the door and nodded as we introduced ourselves. "May we come in?"

This was the moment. If he said "No" or tried to close the door we 'd have to arrest him with just my theory as probable cause. Instead, he nodded, opened the door wide, and said, "Yes."

"Can I get you gentlemen anything?"

Seeing our hesitation – we didn't want him out of sight – Lochner said, "Don't worry, it's upstairs in the closet." After this tacit admission, he added, "I'd feel more comfortable talking over drinks." We followed him into the kitchen. Sitting around his table, we talked and drank – sweet tea for me, Coke for Jook, beer for him.

"Frist one today," he said. "Might be my last one ever."

I took a digital recorder out of my pocket, laid it on the table, and turned it on. "Mr. Lochner, Detective Jook is going to read you your rights. I'm going to talk to you for a moment, then ask you some questions and ask for a statement. The rest will be up to you."

Lochner nodded in understanding. Jook told him about lawyers and staying silent. Then I said,

"My sympathies on the tragic death of your wife. That her death was dismissed as 'incidental' was despicable. I understand that you went to court to change this ruling and your case was rejected. You then tried to bring charges, first criminal then civil, against the organizers of the protest. Again, your complaint was dismissed. 'Collateral damage' is what I believe a lawyer for one of the defendants called Sonya's death. Isn't that so?"

There were tears in Lochner's eyes when he said, "Yeah, that's right."

"So why wait six years?" Jook asked quietly.

"Four years," Lochner corrected. "It was a year before that judge ruled that no one was responsible for my Sonya's death. Four years later, all the TV stations and papers made a big thing about it being five years since Ollie Wallace was killed. They talked about him as if he was some kind of martyr. They talked about the police and what everybody said they did. They talked about the others that were killed, like the kid who got hit by the rock and the woman the window killed.

"I called the stations. I called that guy from *The Truth*, you know, the one who figured out what I was doing, the guy who was almost as smart as you two. No one wanted to talk to me, no one wanted to talk about how them blocking the street the way they did killed Sonya.

"That got me looking on the Internet at the people involved in those demonstrations. Just pictures at first, then I saw some names to put with the pictures."

Lochner's eyes went from sad to cold.

"It took me about a year to make a list of names and addresses. I was in the army and I did some hunting. Always was a damn good shot. Once I got the right kind of gun I decided that more collateral damage was called for."

Lochner took a final sip of his last beer, then gave us a detailed confession for each of the four murders. He told us exactly where his rifle was and that there was a list on his computer with another ten names on it. He finished his statement with,

"Guess they'll listen now."

They listened. TV, the papers, social media, they all listened. Most didn't care. Edward Lochner was portrayed as a man maddened by grief who went on a killing spree. The four men he killed were hailed as martyrs. In that they were killed for a cause they believed in I suppose they were.

Detective Abel Jook received a commendation for his role in the investigation and the arrest. I got yelled at by Alston for involving the BPD and by Linda, Parker, and again by Linda for taking stupid chances. I didn't care. Linda forgave me because she loves me. Parker forgave me because he works for God and so he had to.

Edward Lochner pled guilty. I went to his allocution. It was remorseful and moving and damning all at once. And no one outside Part 7 of the Circuit Court got to hear it. Other than reporting his guilty plea, the media ignored him.

On my way back to my office I thought about Laurel Hanson. Ms. Hanson was the woman who collapsed when Reverend Fells was shot. Despite the valiant effort of Nurse Callie Sutton, Ms. Hanson died on the way to the hospital. Lochner was not charged in her death, as the State was not able to prove that she would not have had the heart attack anyway. I suppose that she was also considered collateral damage and wondered how her loved ones felt about her incidental death.

DUE DILIGENCE

There was no question that Judith Morrow and Leo Harvey had a troubled relationship. At least twice a month, people on either side of their unit, and above and below it, would hear yelling and shouting which would go one for about fifteen or twenty minutes. Then all would be quiet. Sometimes this quiet was followed by moans and sighs but more often not.

No one called the police, not unless the yelling and shouting were followed by screaming and things getting broken. Only then did uniformed members of the Baltimore Police Department respond.

No arrests were ever made. Neither Morrow nor Harvey would press charges against the other. Neither would agree to go to the hospital to be checked out or allow the officers to photograph any obvious injuries. However, in their last visit to the couple's Cold Stream Village apartment, bruising on Morrow's arms and face was briefly recorded by the officers' body cameras until she told them that she was not pressing charges and demanded that they turn the camera off and leave.

Only after a "Are you sure, Ms. Morrow, that you don't want to press charges or be photographed?" and a profanity-laden reply did they leave, turning their cameras off once they were in the hallway.

It was the second to last time that they would be called to apartment 302.

The noise from the apartment above him woke Christopher Jackson at two sixteen in the morning. He knew this because the first thing he did was look at his clock then swear when the blue numbers told him what time it was. How long it had been going on Jackson couldn't say but after five minutes of what sounded like a very good fight, he debated calling the police. However, the last time he had, Harvey later confronted him in the lobby and told him to mind his own damned business. There was an implied "Or else."

"Screw them," Jackson said to his cat Oswald who had crawled up on the bed. He too had been disturbed and had come to his human to complain. Then came the sounds of things breaking.

"Maybe they'll kill each other," Jackson said. But by this time Oswald was no longer interested and had curled up on the bed and gone to sleep. "Good idea," Jackson said and pulled the blankets up. Just then there was a scream followed by a distinct thud.

"Dammit!" As he reached for his phone he noted three minutes had passed.

The BPD responded lights and sirens to Jackson's possible assault in progress 9-1-1 call. He met them at the front door. At his offer to show them to apartment 302 one of them said, "Don't bother, we know the way."

There was no answer to their knock. The responding officers then tried calling both Morrow's and Harvey's phones from a list that Jackson had given them. Still no answer. With a dead quiet coming from inside the apartment and a growing fear that this was more literal than figurative, they decided to force the door.

A few kicks near the doorknob sprang the passage lock. With weapons drawn and mindful of the blood on the apartment door, they carefully went inside.

An unresponsive Leo Harvey was sitting on the living room couch. He was bleeding from a forehead wound and there was blood on his clothes. He did not react to the officers' entry or their drawn pistols or to their unnecessary order not to move. Instead, he simply stared at the body of Judith Morrow, which lay near the table in the dining room.

Officer Velez rushed over to the fallen woman and checked for a pulse. Not finding any, he looked up at his sergeant and shook his head.

Sergeant Deborah Kirk, who had more years in than her three officers combined, began to give orders.

"Call for more units. We'll need this floor taped off." She

pointed to one officer, "Everett, make sure the looky-loos stay in their apartments. And Velez, call dispatch and get an ambo here. Make that two, one for him," she indicated Harvey, "and one to do what's needed."

What was needed was for the EMTs to respond and officially declare the dead woman dead. Mistakes had been made in the past only to be discovered by the Medical Examiner's investigators when they arrived to remove the body. Whether any mistakes had gone as far as the autopsy was something no one even joked about.

"And call Homicide, start them on their way."

"What about the Crime Lab?"

Kirk looked at her watch. The Crime Scene Unit was nearing the end of its tour of duty. *Call them now*, Kirk thought, *and they'll be stuck here for the rest of the night and into the morning. Better to have a fresh crew*. "Let's wait for the warrant, Velez." The sergeant looked down at Morrow. "She's not going anywhere."

Kirk then addressed the third officer, the newest addition to her squad, one who was only six months out of the Police Academy, the one who with a rookie's enthusiasm had been first through the door.

"Copeland, you're the primary on this one." Officer Copeland thought this a good thing, some kind of honor, until he heard Velez let out a sigh of relief. Only then did he realize that he had drawn the short straw. "Stand by here. Start taking notes for your report." Then came the sounds of two kinds of sirens accompanied by red and blue lights which flashed through the window. Back up units and the ambos.

Paramedics arrived. One team declared Judith Morrow dead then left. The other, accompanied by Velez, transported Harvey to Sinai Hospital's ER.

"Write down anything he says," Kirk whispered to Velez, "but don't ask him any questions."

The Homicide Unit arrived. With the memory of what it had been like when she was a rookie, Kirk left Copeland alone with the dead after warning him not to touch anything.

Detective Herbert Morton took the call. The Homicide detective took the domestics whenever he could. Not much OT, but easy to clear. It was always the wife, husband, live-in, or kid. And unlike the real criminals, they were not skilled in murder. The professionals – mostly gangers and dealers – knew how not to leave evidence. No spitting or smoking, wear gloves, pick up your brass or use a revolver, dump or sell the gun. As for witnesses, who cares? This was Baltimore where everyone knew the rule – you could talk or you could live but you couldn't do both.

The amateurs – the mean ones, the ones who lost it, or the ones who didn't care – they left means, motive, and opportunity behind and tried to hide it with a lame-ass story about a break-in or something. And the crime scene guys were very good at spotting fake burglaries because they processed about four thousand of the real things every year.

Morton liked to say he "worked smart, not hard." The truth was, he was lazy and not that smart. If it wasn't for the Crime Lab getting him firearms, latent print, and DNA matches, and the dunker domestics where the killer was practically handed to him, there would be so many red names on the murder board under his name that his lieutenant would be thinking of shipping him back to a district, no matter how close he was to retirement. And Morton did not want to spend his last five months with the BPD on patrol duty in a uniform that no longer fit.

When Morton arrived on the scene he liked what he saw and heard. Locked door, signs of a struggle, his suspect under guard at Sinai. *Hope that cop with him doesn't ask him anything*, he thought as the rookie primary was droning in his ear about bloodstains, prints, and possible weapons.

"Crime Lab stuff," Morton told Officer Copeland. "They know more about that crap than I do." Ignoring the young patrol officer asking about what should be in a primary's report, Morton called the Homicide Office.

"What's keeping the warrant? I need to get out of here and over to Sinai and my suspect. I need to get him out of there before some knucklehead starts asking questions like the last time. …Who's got the duty? … Judge Copper? She's okay. Just make sure to bring her coffee and some Boston Cremes from Dunkin'. Gotta keep the black robes happy."

Morton called for the CSU. A twenty-minute wait on them. They could start before the warrant was signed, just documentation of the scene – photos and sketch – no searching or seizing. Another call, a condition check on the suspect.

"Headwound but not serious, Detective," Officer Velez reported. "He's getting stitched up now. He'll be ready for release in thirty. And yes, I have his clothes. And yes, I have paper overalls for him. And no, he hasn't said anything to me and I haven't asked him anything. "

"Good job," Morton said, making a mental note to talk to the ER staff. Doctor/patient confidentiality was one thing, but having seen too many battered women, some of the staff were sometimes willing to provide some off-the-record info on what the suspect said had happened.

Waiting for the Crime Lab, Morton got what information he needed from Copeland then, because he had time to kill and remembered what it was like on his first murder scene, told the officer what needed to go on the primary's report.

"Go out to your car and get it started. I'll wait with her. Maybe ask her who did it."

A grateful Copeland left, giving Morton time with the body. Just looking, no touching, the Medical Examiner didn't like it when you touched "their" body. He took some shots with his phone and decided that he wouldn't wait on the ME's people. The lab tech would call him if they found anything he needed to know. The rest could wait for the next day's autopsy.

Ninety minutes later, Leo Harvey was in a homicide interview room. He'd been given one of the snacks the Unit bought in bulk at Sam's Club and a cup of coffee. If he didn't take them with him when he left the room the snack packaging and the cup would be submitted for latent print processing and DNA swabbing.

The pros know not to eat or drink, Morton reflected, *or at least to take their trash with them.*

With audio and video recorders running, Morton sat down across the table from Harvey, read him his rights, and began his questioning.

One hour, he thought, making a bet with himself, *one hour and this guy breaks. He wants to tell me what he did.*

"So, Leo, what happened?"

A bleary-eyed Harvey looked back at the detective. "I ... don't remember." He looked at Morton, his eyes blinking as he tried to recall the evening. "We were drinking, her and me, a lot I think. She was there. She wasn't supposed to be. She was supposed to be in Washington. But she was there. There was ... a fight. We yelled. She yelled, I yelled, she yelled. She pushed me and I fell. I got up. She hit me with ... something and I fell again." Harvey rubbed his stitches. There were ten of them. He'd probably wind up with a Harry Potter scar. "Then she ... she was going to hit ... I got up, she ... pushed. She hit the table, fell hard. Then she was gone. I got on the sofa."

Harvey closed his eyes tight a few times, as if remembering what he had done. Or maybe it was because the meds hadn't fully kicked in and his head wound hurt. Then he went silent and just stared at Morton.

"What happened then?" the detective prompted.

"Cops woke me up."

Morton thought about what Harvey had just said. He checked his notes. "Okay, Leo, let's go over this. You correct me if I'm wrong. You and Judy ..."

"Er, Judith. She hated Judy."

And you probably did too, Morton thought but didn't say. But that correction would show that Harvey was aware of what was going on. "You and Judith. You were drinking, you got to fighting. She hit you, you pushed her into the table and killed her. Is that right?"

To Leo Harvey that sounded right, almost. There was something missing but he wasn't sure. He didn't remember. With the drink, the drugs, and the pain he just didn't remember.

On TV, the detective sometimes makes the suspect write out

their confession. Or the detective would have it written out for them to sign. Morton didn't like that. Putting it on paper, seeing it on paper, that sometimes gave the suspect time to think. And thinking is the last thing Morton wanted his suspect to do. That's why, in addition to the room's recording devices, he always kept his body cam on.

After placing Leo Harvey under arrest for murder and putting him in a holding cell to await transport to Central Booking, Morton called the crime lab working his scene.

"April, check the dining room table. Our guy said he pushed her head into it."

"Already done, Detective. Blood and hair on the corner. ME says it looks like it matches her head wound."

"You're going to recover the table, right? It is the murder weapon."

"Go to hell, Morton. Listen." The sound of a circular saw came over his phone. "We're cutting out the piece we need. ME's going to sign for it so the doctor can compare it to the wound during the autopsy. That means you get to recover and submit it."

April laughed and hung up.

Morton didn't get too upset at the dump job. It was a game they all played. Looking at his watch, he saw that he had won his bet – less than an hour from Miranda to arrest.

I didn't know Leo Harvey or Judith Morrow. I had never even heard of them. Few people had. Morrow's death occurred after the eleven o'clock news so no camera crews came out. With no footage, it was neither live nor late-breaking. *The Baltimore Sun* mentioned her passing in one paragraph on page 7, along with what number homicide she was that year. To them, she was barely news, just a statistic. *The Baltimore Truth* did not even mention her. Neither had any family members been willing to stand before TV cameras wearing T-shirts reading "Justice for Judith" or "Free Leo."

Despite the lack of media interest, Harvey's trial got fast-tracked. A quick indictment and an early court date. That's why the case folder came across my desk. Part of my job as Special

Investigator for the State's Attorney's Office was to examine crime scene reports, photographs, recovered forensic evidence, and any comparisons and analyses.

In the case of the State vs. Leo Harvey, the photos looked good and matched what was written in the report. Recovered from the scene were latent prints, blood samples, an "art deco" statue" with "visible ridge detail" in blood, and a piece of drywall bearing a visible palmprint – also in blood. The palm was found low to the floor, just above the baseboard. There was also a piece of wood cut from the corner of a dining room table. (I used to love doing stuff like that when I was a crime scene tech.) The Medical Examiner's report stated that the piece of table was "consistent with the deceased's wound" and that impact with the corner piece was the likely cause of death.

And that was all. There were no comparisons of the latent prints found on the table, the apartment door, or the glasses and bottles found on the scene. Nor were there comparisons with either of the bloody visible prints to Harvey's. There is no more damning evidence against a defendant than their print in the victim's blood. At the least, this should have been done. But it wasn't. Nor was there any serology work.

There could have been any number of reasons why no further forensics had been done. The Lab is notoriously backed up. I suspect that some of the latent prints I lifted when I worked crime scenes were still in someone's stack of pending cases. Another reason is that Detective Morton was notoriously slack in requesting analyses, especially when he's got a dunker with a confession.

Still, you want to go into court with your best evidence. So I wrote up requests asking for DNA analysis and print comparisons in the Harvey case, with priority to be given to the visible prints on the statue and the cut out drywall. In my emailed request, I mentioned that the trial was coming up within a month and asked for the work to be expedited. Then I went on to the next case and forgot all about Leo Harvey.

Two days later my request came back with a big, fat "DENIED" in bright red, uppercase letters. No reasons were given so I called the Laboratory Division to get some.

"Grace," said Stewart Burris, supervisor of the Latent Print Unit, "we've got real cases to worry about. And before you give me the usual 'every case is important, every victim deserves justice' whine I'll have you know that Herb Morton agrees. In fact, he's the one who told me that this case didn't need to be worked and that we should concentrate on the whodunnits and stone-cold murders instead of wasting our time on a gimme case with a confession."

I got the same, almost word-for-word reply from Gloria Jennings, the head of the Serology Unit.

One more step. I called Barbara Horowitz, the Assistant State's Attorney who was assigned to the Harvey case.

"Ms. Horowitz, Matthew Grace here."

"Yes, what is it, Mr. Grace?"

"Just a heads up," I said, then told her about the lack of analyses and comparisons on her case.

There was a noticeable pause before she answered. "Yes, I know. Don't worry about it. They won't, er, be needed."

"Making a deal then?"

"Yeah, something like that." She gave a nervous laugh then said, "Thanks anyway."

A plea bargain, that explained things. I pictured the pretrial meeting in my mind. Horowitz opened with a confession and a history of domestic violence. Harvey's attorney may have called with a self-defense argument. Then Horowitz went all-in with the potential damning prints in blood evidence and the defense mucked its cards.

Having done my job and followed up on it, I once again moved on to other cases, telling myself that not everything was a mystery for a bored special investigator to solve.

I would have forgotten all about Judith Morrow and Leo Harvey had Sharon Manchester, my immediate boss, not poked her head into my office the next day and asked,

"Matthew, what's your interest in the Harvey case. Celina says you've been bothering people about it."

I should have expected that. Horowitz was one of the ASAs

Alston counted on to get convictions in well-publicized cases. She was probably on the phone to Alston as soon as I hung up.

I shrugged. "Just due diligence." I explained what I had done and why. Sharon seemed satisfied and left me to my work. She also left me wondering why the State's Attorney for Baltimore City was interested in a below the media domestic murder case and why she had given it to one of her top guns.

I decided not to worry about her, or Harvey. His lawyer could have asked the same questions I had, could have demanded the comparisons and analyses I had requested. They didn't, going for the sure thing instead of rolling the dice. Once again, I decided to forget about the whole thing, at least until the trial.

The case of the State of Maryland vs. Leo Jerome Harvey was called two months later with me in the gallery. It was my first time in a courtroom since that juror got killed. I don't know why I was there. A quick plea, a sentence handed down, and on to the next case.

Judge Raymond Kelly – Judge Hanover's replacement – was still in his chambers. Barbara Horowitz and Bailey Doyle, Harvey's public defender, were in an animated discussion up front. She looked upset, he looked apologetic. I heard a whispered "We had a deal" come from her and a "When can I do? He wants a trial" from him.

Judge Kelly came in. We stood, His Honor sat, we sat, and the bailiff did his thing. Harvey was brought in, his handcuffs and shackles not going well with his new suit.

The suit bothered me. Why would his lawyer get him all dressed up for a plea? The sheriff's deputies took off his chains, Harvey sat down next to Doyle, and Judge Kelly called for the jury.

Jury? I took a closer look at the counsel for the defense.

He was young, maybe eighteen months out of law school, maybe a year in the District Courts taking pleas and gaining experience trying mostly unwinnable cases.

No wonder Horowitz was upset. This new guy, this "kid" had sandbagged her. He had worked out a guilty plea and now, after taking a closer look at the evidence – or lack thereof – he was going to trial, ready to point out all the things that weren't done in the BPD's and prosecution's "rush to judgment."

And there was nothing the State, as represented by Barbara Horowitz, could do about it.

You should have listened to me, Barb, I thought in a mental "I told you so." *This is Baltimore, Hon, and the only thing you can count on is that you can't count on anything.*

Horowitz put on what little case she had – the locked door, the fight, the piece of table, and lastly Harvey's confession, making it all sound as damning as the prints in blood nobody cared about.

Christopher Jackson testified about his calling the police and why. Officer Copeland talked about forcing the door and described the scene. The ME came and gave the cause and time of death. Then it was Detective Morton's turn.

He glossed over the CSU's activities, mentioning that the crime scene tech had taken photographs, drawn a sketch, and recovered evidence. Yes, he told the judge and jury, the photos and the sketch were fair and accurate representations of the scene. None of the evidence was produced or even mentioned.

Despite Doyle's half-hearted objection, the video of Harvey's confession was played for the jury. I don't know about his peers but it all sounded a little off to me, a little incoherent, and with too many pronouns.

Horowitz milked things for a long as she could before turning Morton over to the defense.

The catchphrase of The Nightmare, my favorite pulp character, came to mind. *Time to play*, I thought, as I smiled in anticipation of Doyle's questioning. Why weren't the prints compared? Why was there no blood analysis? Could Leo Harvey have been defending himself? And best of all, when questioned, Leo Harvey was in pain, medicated and drunk – hospital records put his blood alcohol level at 0.24 – isn't it likely that he wasn't in his right mind when questioned?

PD Doyle asked none of these questions. In fact, other than asking why the table wasn't recovered, he didn't ask any questions.

Has this been TV, at Doyle's "Nothing further," an excited murmur would have run through the seated crowd but there were only six of us in the gallery and if the other five were as shocked and disappointed as I was they didn't show it. The judge was though, you could tell by his face.

Judge Kelly was new. Had it been Judge Gertrude Deveraux behind the bench she would have asked all the questions Doyle had not. Instead, all he asked was, "Are you sure, Mr. Doyle?"

"Yes, Your Honor. Nothing further, Your Honor."

With that, the prosecution rested.

"Your Honor, the defense calls Leo Harvey."

Doyle led his client to the stand where Harvey either swore or affirmed that he would tell the truth, the whole truth, and nothing but the truth under penalty of perjury. (God plays no part in Maryland courts. Make of that what you will.)

"Mr. Harvey, please tell us, to the best of your recollection, what happened on the night Judith Morrow died."

Harvey was an average-sized man, not big, not small. But on the stand, he looked small, small and scared. And why not? When this trial was over, everyone but him would go on with their lives. If convicted, Harvey's life as he knew it was over.

Small, nervous, and scared. No doubt the jury saw it too. And maybe they pitied him, or maybe they thought it was the look of a guilty man.

"The truth is, I have no recollection of what happened. I remember going home after a party …"

"Where was this party?" Doyle asked.

"In the building. I drank a lot at the party. When I got home I drank some more. The next thing I remember is being in the hospital. After that, being locked up in Central Booking."

"Do you remember waiving your rights or confessing to Detective Morton?"

"No sir, I do not."

"Did you kill Judith Morrow?"

Here Harvey paused, and a well-rehearsed pause it seemed to be, then looked at the jury and said, "I don't know. I don't remember.

I really wish I did."

Horowitz tried to cross-examine Harvey but Doyle objected to most of her questions with "Mr. Harvey has said he doesn't remember."

Frustrated, she sat down. With that, the defense, such as it was, rested.

In his closing argument, Doyle argued that the jury should disregard Harvey's confession because he was not fully able to waive his rights and was highly vulnerable to suggestion. He then argued that the crime scene led as much to self-defense as it did to manslaughter. He closed with, "Members of the jury, if Leo Harvey cannot be sure of what happened that night, how can you be?"

Barbara Horwitz countered by reminding the jurors of what facts there were in the case. That Judith Morrow was dead and Leo Harvey was not. She reminded the jury that, yes, he had been drinking but he had confessed. "*In vino veritas*," she quoted, "in wine lies the truth."

Horowitz finished up by pointing out to the jury that just because Leo Harvey could not remember killing Judith Morrow, that doesn't mean he didn't. "Being blind drunk does not excuse one's actions. It does not excuse murder."

I learned later that it took the jury a little over three hours to convict Leo Harvey of voluntary manslaughter for which he could receive a sentence of up to ten years.

Poor bastard, I thought when I heard the verdict. *Had he had a better lawyer he might now be free.* I then gave a thought to Judith Morrow. However long a sentence Harvey receives, she got the death penalty. I thought about the evidence that wasn't examined and wondered if it would have made a difference. Either way, every death had to be paid for and Leo Harvey had been given the bill.

The mind is a funny thing. It not only stores information, it keeps on processing it even when you're not aware it's doing so. It was about ten days after Leo Harvey had been found guilty. My wife Linda and I were grocery shopping. At the checkout, the cashier said, "The chip reader is broken, you'll have to swipe your card."

The word "swipe" has different meanings. You swipe left or right to reject or choose someone on Tinder. If you take something without paying you "swipe" it. You swipe your credit card to pay for something you want.

Swipe has a forensic meaning as well. In bloodstain analysis, it indicates a stain caused by something with blood on it coming into contact with a clean surface.

As I said, the mind keeps working. When the cashier said "swipe" my mind took me back to the Harvey case, back to the unexamined bloodstains in the apartment, back to the bloodstain on the outside of the apartment door. The door that had to be forced because it was locked. If Morrow was dead and Harvey virtually passed out on the sofa, who had left the stain? One explanation was that at some time Harvey had opened and closed the door. Another was that there had been someone else in the apartment when Morrow was killed.

Unlike certain TV detectives, I did not abandon my wife and immediately rush off to re-examine the photographs. It was Friday evening and we had plans for the weekend. The evidence would wait until Monday. It wasn't going anywhere. Neither were Harvey or Morrow for that matter.

Monday came. I spent the morning doing the work the State's Attorney's Office pays me to do. As I reviewed reports and looked at crime scene photos I kept thinking about a bloodstain on a door and what I was going to do about it.

The case was closed. The trial had been held and twelve people had declared Leo Harvey guilty. Who was I to say he wasn't? If I opened the Morrow case file, if I called up the photos, I might find nothing or I might find the truth of what happened, and from everything I'd seen about this case, nobody involved but Harvey cared about that.

What was it Burris said, something about every victim deserving justice? Was it justice for Judith Morrow if the wrong person went to jail for her death?. Was it justice for Leo Harvey if he were that wrong person? And who was I to dispense that justice? Did I want to walk down that road again?

A saying about Evil and good men doing nothing went through my mind.

To Hell with it, I thought and accessed the file I'd been thinking about all weekend.

It's a swipe, I decided as I looked at the bloodstain. It was on the exterior latch side of the door, going toward the hinge side. Whoever left it was going out, not in. There were no blood drops on the floor on either side of the door, and no drops in the hallway, so they weren't hurt, or rather, they weren't badly bleeding. The crime scene tech had measured it (at least someone had done their job) and it was four foot eight inches from the floor – about shoulder or upper sleeve height.

I looked at photos taken of Morrow on the scene and Harvey after his "confession." There was blood on his shirt and pants from his head wound, but none on his arms. He would have had to have smashed into the door to leave any kind of a stain and that would not have been a swipe. Morrow had a fatal head wound and she had not gone anywhere after hitting the table. In addition, she didn't any blood on her arms either.

There was a strong possibility that a third person had been involved. If so, why hadn't Harvey mentioned him or her? Or maybe he had. When listening to his recorded confession in court I had thought there had been too many pronouns.

I pulled up a transcript of what Harvey had said. No names, just pronouns. We assumed that they all referred to the same person. I thought *what if* and rewrote it using my sister's name in addition to Morrow's.

"We were drinking, Susan and me, a lot I think. Judith was there. She wasn't supposed to be. She was supposed to be in Washington. But Judith was there. There was … a fight. We yelled. Judith yelled, I yelled, Susan yelled. Judith pushed me and I fell. I got up. Judith hit me with … something and I fell again. Then Judith … she was going to hit … I got up, Susan … pushed. Judith hit the table, fell hard. Then Susan was gone. I got on the sofa."

That made more sense, to me at least. Probably not to anyone who wanted the case to go away.

I looked further into the case folder. It hadn't been mentioned in court because it wasn't needed but the Cold Stream Village apartments had outdoor video surveillance and Sergeant Kirk had thought to get a copy. I pulled it up and played it. No one had left the building from an hour before Christopher Jackson had been woken up to the time the police arrived. The third person, if there was a third person, probably lived in the building.

Four floors, eight apartments per floor, thirty-two apartments less one. Not a job for one guy poking into something that no one wants poked. I had to narrow things down.

Apartment management was happy to supply the SAO with a list of its tenants. "Routine follow-up" I explained. The building manager guessed it had something to do with Harvey's sentencing hearing and I didn't correct him.

Thirty-one apartments, over seventy residents that management knew about. Again, too much work for someone who's been neglecting his real job for most of the morning. Still, I looked over the name, concentrating on the female ones. Halfway down the list, I came to Leila Resnick.

That name was familiar. None of the others were. Resnick lived alone in a fourth-floor apartment. I looked her up. There weren't many of them with that spelling.

One lived in California. One had died two years ago in Omaha and her family had sprung for a very nice tombstone. A third was listed as having been an executive vice-president of the now-closed Charm City Shred-It company.

Some of Charm City Shred-It's employees had not been immediately shredding the documents they picked up from businesses and offices. They first reviewed them, looking for information to sell. Information like the names of witnesses in murder cases.

That was the case that got me back into the game of cops and robbers. Acting for the State's Attorney's Office I had exposed the scheme but no one from the company had been tried or even arrested. That might or might not have had something to do with the President of Charm City Shred-It, Leslie Resnick, being an old college friend of Celina Alston. A few months ago Celina had questioned my involvement in the Leo Harvey case. Now I knew why.

It didn't take long to determine that Leslie and Leila Resnick were sisters. I ran what might have happened in my head.

Thinking Morrow was out of town, Leila and Harvey were drinking in his apartment, maybe a prelude to doing more than drinking. An unexpected Morrow comes in. There's a fight. Harvey gets hurt, Leila does some pushing, Morrow gets dead. Leila gets blood on her sleeve or shoulder, either from Morrow or Harvey. She runs out of the apartment, leaving the swipe on the door. She waits for the knock on the door, for Harvey to give her up. But in his condition he mostly forgets about her. When the knock doesn't come, she calls Leslie who then calls Alston, possibly hinting that if Leila does get involved, the Charm City Shred-It mess may come out, including Alston's role in the cover-up. Thinking what's one more poor bastard after several dead witnesses, Alston agrees.

Sitting alone in my office, it made sense to me, a lot of sense. Unfortunately, something making sense is not evidence.

This is why I was hesitant to walk this road. There was still a chance to turn back. If I did, I knew I'd be haunted by a man I had never met, one who might spend years in jail for something he may not have done, all because I was like the others and didn't care what happened to him. If I went forward, I'd tick off a lot of people and probably lose my job.

Long ago I sinned. In an act of hubris, I framed a man for a murder he didn't commit so that he would be punished for those he had gotten away with. I got caught and lost my job but was never really punished.

Maybe this was my long-delayed penance. If it was, then so be it.

I spent my lunch hour and most of the afternoon working on how to prove my suspicions. I decided that the next day I was going to see a judge about some court orders. But first I called Lieutenant

Joshua Parker.

"Hello, Grace, you're not calling for Her, are you?"

"No, Deacon, She might be involved but I'm doing this on my own. And I'm calling to tell you that one of your detectives might be in the jackpot."

"Which one?" he asked, his friendly voice dropping to a growl. Parker takes it personally when his detectives misbehave.

"Herbert Morton," I said.

"He's not mine. He works a different shift, thank the Lord," he said, his voice almost back to normal. "And he doesn't even work that anymore. He's been detailed to the SAO until his retirement after which he'll be your coworker until he messes up and She fires him. What's he done? Is it the Morrow case?"

"You knew about that?"

"Grace, you should know by now that I know everything."

"Then why didn't you do anything?"

"Knowing and being able to do something about what you know are two different things. I did do some praying on it, though."

"And what happened?"

"This phone call. I knew I was right when I got you into the SAO."

This time my requests for DNA analysis and print comparisons in the Judith Morrow case were not only accepted, they were prioritized thanks to a court order from Judge Devereaux. Her Honor had listened to my theories and had agreed with them. She also issued a gag order as well, thus making sure that Alston would not find out. If she did, I warned Laboratory Director Thomas Kendall, someone was getting one of Her Honor's contempt goodie bags and a thirty-day vacation at the Lockup Hotel and Spa.

DNA analysis takes a week or two. Print comparisons come back fast. So I had the results from the latent and visible prints before the Lab's Serology Unit was even close to working up a profile. The bloody detail on the statue was blood but it wasn't a print, just part of the statue's pattern. The Latent Print Unit did process the statue, however, and came up with Judith Morrow's print just where one would grab it to hit somebody. The palm on the drywall – that was a suitable print and it matched Leo Harvey's right hand.

That made sense. Judith hit him, he went down. He rubbed his wound, then pushed off the wall with his bloody hand.

The prints on the bottles and glasses belonged to Harvey and Leila Resnick. A thumbprint on the inner latchside of the apartment door was also hers.

She was there. Leila Resnick was in the apartment when things went down. And nobody knew about her presence on the scene because people did not do their jobs. Detective Morton forgot that when you investigate a crime you do so believing that everything you suspect is true while at the same time you believe nothing is true. Two of the Lab's analytical unit rejected requests from an SAO investigator who maybe should have pushed a little harder when they did. Barbara Horowitz would probably do anything Alston wanted. Then again, if you have a plea deal you don't worry about evidence. As for Public Defender Baily Doyle's tanking the defense – maybe it was inexperience or maybe something else. Morton seems to have received his reward. I wondered what Doyle was offered. I'd know when I asked him.

I made some of what we investigators call "discrete inquiries' and found out that Doyle frequented Clancy's on the Avenue. I know a bartender who works there so I arranged for him to call me when the PD showed up. Two days later I got the call.

I slipped into Doyle's booth just as he finished his dinner.

"Who are you?"

"Matthew Grace, investigator for the State's Attorney's Office." Before he could ask what I wanted I showed him my badge. "What did they offer you to help convict Leo Harvey?"

Looks of worry and fear crossed his face. I felt sorry for him. He was new and inexperienced, maybe trying to do the right thing but, given that a good number of his clients were less than upstanding citizens, he wasn't quite sure what that was. Now there was a cop flashing a badge and asking if he were part of a criminal conspiracy.

"Look," I told him, "tell me the truth and whatever it is stays at this table. Lie to me and your name shows up in *The Baltimore Truth* in ways you and your boss won't like. Now, what was the deal?"

Doyle hesitated, wrestling with his conscience. "They told me …"

"Who told you?" I took an educated guess. "Barbara Horowitz?"

His surprise showed that I had guessed right. Alston would not have wanted another person added to the mix. Doyle's look changed to relief as my knowing this allowed his conscience to win. "She showed me a list of my next twenty cases. She told me that I could expect half of those cases to be *nolle prossed.* For the rest, I would get either generous plea deals or light sentences."

"Which would make you look good. And all you had to do was let Leo Harvey go to jail."

Doyle nodded, then his head dropped in what I hoped was shame.

"You betrayed your client, Doyle. You betrayed the Law. You betrayed yourself." I handed him an envelope.

"What's this?"

"Redemption, maybe for Harvey, definitely for you. It's the discovery you should have asked for and the test results you should have demanded. Use it to petition Judge Deveraux for a new trial. I have it on good authority that she'll grant you one. If you're asked where you got the information, fall back on privilege or plead the Fifth. Just don't mention my name because I was never here and I can prove it."

Leo Harvey was granted a new trial. It never happened. Instead, the State of Maryland in the person of Barbara Horowitz dropped all charges against him.

Leila Resnick's name was not mentioned in court or in public so Alston got what she wanted. And because the case never hit the paper, all those people who didn't do their jobs got to keep them.

Except maybe me.

The day after Harvey walked out of court a free man Alston summoned me to her office.

"I think you went further than due diligence in the Leo Harvey case, Grace."

"Just doing my job as best I can, Ms. Alston." I handed her my case folder, which did not mention my meeting with Bailey Doyle.

"I don't want that."

I put the folder under my arm with a "Yes, Ma'am. Should I file it or … shred it?"

Alston's blue eyes grew dark. "Grace, do you know the meaning of 'at will employment'?" she asked.

"Yes, ma'am," I answered. "I was thinking that one day I'd discuss that with Murphy of *The Baltimore Truth*."

Here it comes, I thought as her face reddened in anger. Instead, she gained control of herself and snarled (yes, she really snarled), "Get out."

So I got to keep my job as well. For how long I didn't know. What I did know was that it was time to start thinking about a career in hotel security.

IN THE MIX

The numbered men gathered around him, like Roman Senators on the Ides of March. Sharp weapons were in their hands, mostly prison-made but some smuggled in from the outside. They closed in slowly, blocking the view of the correctional officers who weren't watching anyway.

It wasn't supposed to be like this, Morgan Uris said to himself as the men came closer. *It was supposed to be isolation then Club Fed, a new name, protective custody. Not gen-pop in a real prison, not in the mix.*

They knew him for what he was, or rather, what he had been. And not one of them liked him for it. What they liked was that it was payback time and damn the consequences.

He looked into their faces and they let him; it wasn't as if he was going to be able to identify them later. He knew them all, especially the one who led them. He had been someone Uris had been friendly with in the past, someone for whom he cut a few breaks. *You too*, he thought, unconsciously echoing what were believed to be Caesar's last words.

The mob closed in. Arms thrust forward. Hands rose and fell. Morgan Uris felt the sharp things enter him over and over, felt his life drain away. Soon he went down.

It was only after Uris fell and the men began to disperse that the COs moved in. Prisoners scattered; knives, sharpened toothbrushes, homemade razors, and assorted other DIY weaponry were dropped.

As Uris's body lay still, the COs called in the attack and the prison went on lockdown. Cells would be searched and weapons recovered, none of which would have Uris's blood on them.

Medics arrived and rushed the fallen man to the infirmary but it was too late. At 9:15 am, the morning after his transfer from protective custody into the prison's general population, Morgan

Uris, once a police officer and now a convicted felon, was dead.

His death made the news, just as his trial had several months ago. I felt sorrow at his death. Yes, he had broken the law. Yes, he deserved to be punished. But he did not deserve to die.

Part of me felt responsible for what had happened to him. As the State Attorney's Special Investigator I had investigated him for abduction and murder and found sufficient evidence to charge him. But this was balanced by the fact that later I found the person he was supposed to have murdered alive and well and living in North Carolina.

But this did not take him off Celina Alston's radar.

"Grace," Alston had told me when I started the investigation, "Morgan Uris is a violent thug with a badge, one with multiple complaints of excessive force, some of which fit the legal definition of aggravated assault."

Having no sympathy for the bad cops who stained the honor of the rest of the department, I had suggested that she request his body cam footage. "Have it reviewed, all of it. It's a boring job so get someone whose last name is other than Grace to do it. If it shows him abusing his position or improperly turning off the camera, charge him."

So there, I had dropped him into the mix and I had gotten him out again, got him a second chance. A chance to make up for the violent behavior that had caused Janis Bray to frame him for her murder. A chance to make up for his abusive actions as a patrol officer on the streets of Baltimore. A chance to make things right.

I had told him as much. He had come to see me a few days after being released from Central Booking where he was being held without bail pending his trial.

"Sorry about calling you a mother-raper. You were just doing your job," he said over lunch at Potbelly's.

I nodded an okay and asked, "How'd you get into Chester Himes?"

"I saw the movies with Godfrey Cambridge. When I found out they were from books I read some. Good stuff."

We talked Chester Himes for a bit, he hadn't heard about Njami

Simon's *Coffin & Co.* so I gave him a rundown and he said he'd look for it. When we talked out that subject I said,

"I meant what I said about Celina Alston targeting you. Going after cops is the horse she hopes to ride to City Hall. You're now in her sights and from what I know about her, you're one of the ones who got away. She's got a volunteer detail of social activists reviewing random body-cam footage and I wouldn't be surprised if your number kept coming up." Then I added, "But you didn't hear that from me."

"Hear what from you? All I heard was about some French guy who wrote a book and how Himes once wrote a sex comedy. But thanks for the heads-up. And for what it's worth, I think you're right. From now on, it's by-the-book and no cutting corners."

Uris kept his word. For six months there was no better cop in the BPD. His arrests went down but the ones he made stuck. Complaints against him dropped to zero and his body-cam footage could have been used in the Academy to train cadets on how to interact with the public.

If only he had not had a social life.

One would have thought that having a girlfriend deliberately drop off the gird and frame him for her murder would have taught Uris a lesson on how not to treat women. As he had with Janis Bray, Uris met Connie Royson on the job. This time she was not a DUI to whom he had given a break but a burglary victim. Uris responded to her house for a break-in a month after I found Janis. In another month they were dating. Two months later there was a knock-down, drag-out fight in which Uris had done most of the hitting. Royson obtained an *ex parte* order against him and had him arrested for physical and sexual assault.

The sexual assault aspect of the case was questionable. There was no reason to doubt that it happened but there was no physical evidence that said it did. But Royson's injuries were such that the Grand Jury had no problem indicting Uris for the physical attack, just as a jury of his peers had no trouble in convicting him. Nor did the presiding judge hesitate in sentencing Uris to fifteen years for first degree aggravated assault. The sentence might have been less but Connie Royson's victim impact statement was a thing a beauty and Janis Bray's testimony during the sentencing hearing of how she faked her death to escape Uris sealed the deal.

So Uris went away for his sins against Connie Royson and, in part, against Janis Bray. And paid for those sins with his life.

Uris was buried in a small cemetery just off of the O'Donnell Street exit off I-95. The service lacked the ceremony and honors an ex-cop usually receives after his death. No Honor Guard, no long procession of fellow officers, no mournful bagpipes playing "Amazing Grace." I went because Lieutenant Joshua Parker asked me to accompany him. He went because, as he put it, "Someone has to bear witness, Grace." So we stood at his graveside with the minister, Uris's sister, and, surprisingly, Janis Bray and her father Nicholas.

After the last prayer was said I went over to the Brays. "Mr. Bray, Ms. Bray. I must confess that I'm surprised to see you here."

She muttered a hello. He shook my offered hand and replied, "As we are you, Mr. Grace."

"Uris was a man who was given a second chance and wasted it. I'm here mourning that waste. Why are you two here?"

"First of all, Mr. Grace, I don't believe in second chances. As to why I'm here, after what that bastard did to Janis, what he drove her to do, I just want to make sure that the son of a bitch is dead. Now if you'll excuse us."

Judge Cordelia Copper had called Bray a vindictive man. It looked like he was, blaming Uris for what his daughter did to the man, putting her sins on him. I supposed it was Uris's fault that Janis had stolen several hundred thousand dollars from one of her daddy's offshore accounts, or that after I found her she disappeared again. Apparently, they had made up. I wonder if he let her keep the money.

I wanted to stick around to see how vindictive Bray was, if he'd wait until everyone left then slip the gravedigger a few bucks to turn away long enough for him to pee on Uris's coffin. But Parker was buying lunch, and I wasn't going to miss that.

The cemetery wasn't too far from Canton Crossing, a large strip mall/restaurant complex on Boston Street. Since it was his treat I let him pick the restaurant and we walked into Mission BBQ minutes before noon, in time for the daily singing of the Star-Spangled Banner. Of course we sang along, with me and everyone other than Parker shouting out the "Oh" of the second to the last line in support of the Baltimore Orioles.

Parker got the brisket and a side of mac and cheese. I got turkey and fries. We ate most of our meal in silence, then, over refills of sweet tea, he said,

"Uris wasn't supposed to die."

"I thought, Deacon, that we are all supposed to die."

"In the Lord's appointed time, Grace, and it may be that this was the time He had chosen for the man. But Uris was not supposed to be out of protective custody and in the mix."

"Why not?"

"Grace, what I'm about to tell you goes no further." I nodded agreement and Parker went on. "After his conviction, Uris made a deal with the Feds."

I immediately thought back to a man who called himself "Smith." I was hoping that Uris hadn't made a similar deal to trade bodies for time off.

"In addition to my duties in Homicide," Parker went on, "I've been assigned to a special task force investigating corruption in the department, and I am not speaking of bullies with a badge like Uris. This appears to be organized. As of yet, we don't know how far it's spread. It may be only a handful of cops. Or it may be department-wide, with officers and detectives in districts and specialized units. We don't know, yet. We do know that some of the drug gangs are involved, as is the Baltimore mob."

I tried not to think about the man I call "Mr. Louis." Instead, I asked, "How did Uris fit in?"

"Uris was a bad cop but he wasn't a crooked one. He was a misogynistic racist who liked beating on people but there's no evidence that he ever took a dime he didn't legally earn. But he had a reputation, and because of it, he was approached more than once with the opportunity 'to get in on a good thing.' He turned them down but, being the kind of cop he was, he never said anything about it."

"Until he was facing a hard fifteen."

"Exactly, Grace. The day after his sentence was handed down he had his lawyer call the Feds. In exchange for minimum security, a new identity, and no more than five years, he'd give up the names of the officers who had approached him as well as telling what he had heard about what they were doing and who was doing it. But he wound up dead before he could be transferred."

"Somebody knew, and that someone called in a favor," I said.

"We're looking into everybody from the top down. Warden Betty Dreyer denies knowing anything about it."

"But she might be lying."

"Everyone lies, Grace. That's the first thing you learn on this job."

"What do you need from me?"

"Grace, you have a way of looking at cases that sometimes amazes me. And, frankly, your solutions to these cases sometimes scare me. You may not find anything but just look into this for me."

"For you, Deacon, anything."

On the parking lot, Parker asked, "How much longer do you place to keep working for Her?"

"Maybe not much longer. Andre Henderson, the head of security at the hotel Linda manages, has finally put in his papers. He plans to retire in four months. I have two months to decide if I want the job. Of course, Alston might just fire me tomorrow."

"I'm surprised she hasn't already." We reached our cars. As Parker got into his he said, "And the next time you talk to him, tell your friend Mr. Louis that we're only after cops. For now." Then he drove off.

I wasn't surprised that he knew about my association with the now-retired head of the Baltimore mob. He was Parker, of course he knew.

On the way home I did some thinking about the case.

Someone had ordered Uris into the mix. Warden Betty Dreyer

could have. Or an administrative clerk could have been paid to alter the orders or change a name. Or a CO working for themselves. While most are decent people working a dangerous job for not enough money, there are other COs who supplement their pay by passing messages, smuggling things in and out, or maybe moving a prisoner from a safe area to a more dangerous one.

This sort of thing is not something you do via email or anything else that leaves a trace. If you're smart, you use burner phones, intermediaries, or go face to face. But if you were smart, you'd know that that you had to get away with it every time and that it only took one slip-up to bring you down.

But some people are not that smart. They tell themselves that they won't get caught *this time*. And they're right, until the last time. Then it all falls down.

So where could I go to find the person who was not that smart? Fortunately, the Fairfield Detention Center had done the job for me.

In her public report on the killing of Morgan Uris, Warden Dreyer stated that everyone who had the authority to order someone transferred into the general population had been questioned and cleared. Uris's "unfortunate death" was deemed the result of a series of mistaken identities and clerical errors and that an investigative committee would be formed to determine how to prevent such errors in the future. The report ended by expressing the Department of Corrections' sympathy to Uris's loved ones.

As public reports go, it did a splendid job of saying nothing. But then it didn't have to. Uris was a cop gone bad and no one except his sister loved him.

Working in the State's Attorney's office I was able to get the full report, the one that listed the names of those who could order transfers – from Dreyer herself down to the Correctional Supervisors. Also listed were the COs who were on duty in both the protective and general wards. There were less than a dozen in all. I'd start with them and try to narrow the list down to one. But before doing that, I decided to visit Mr. Lewis.

That Saturday I bought two cheesecakes from the Woodlea Bakery and drove to a private care facility in northeast Baltimore

County.

The facility in which Mr. Louis lives is partly assisted living, partly nursing home, and partly private hospital. It is very expensive and very exclusive.

When I was escorted to his room, Mr. Lewis was in his rocker recliner.

"Mr. Grace, how are you?"

I paused to take a look at him. He was smaller and paler than when I last saw him. Physically he seemed weaker. It was hard to believe that once upon a time the frail old man before me could, with a word, cause anyone in the city and surrounding counties to disappear.

"I'm fine, Mr. Louis. What about you?"

He let out a long sigh of resignation. "The doctors no longer bring me good news. They've even stopped talking about treatments. Instead, they talk about advanced directives, wills, and keeping me comfortable in the time I have left. Is that cheesecake?"

"From Woodlea's."

"Where else?" As I put the two packages in his mini-fridge he asked,

"So is this a personal visit or has Miss Alston's special investigator finally found enough evidence against this old gangster?"

"Mr. Louis, if I wanted to arrest you, you would already be behind bars."

He laughed and gestured to a chair. When I sat he said, "Better men than you have tried, Mr. Grace, and they've all come up short. Maybe I'll leave you my memoirs in my will so you'll know just how much I've gotten away with."

"I hope it will be many years before I read it."

"Don't lie to a dying old man, Mr. Grace."

"Lying is one of the things I do best, Mr. Louis. If you want the truth, the next time I come I'll bring Joshua Parker."

Mr. Louis knew the name. "The last honest man in Baltimore. How is the lieutenant?'

"He's fine. How secure is this room?"

"You can confess what you like in here, Mr. Grace. You'll only be heard by me and God. And now, my son, what sins are you about to commit?"

"I bring a warning." Mr. Louis's eyes narrowed as I told him about Parker's task force. "Your people are not targets, not yet. That could change if there's no progress."

He nodded in understanding. "As you know, Mr. Grace, I have no people. But I do have friends, friends who are always willing to cooperate with the law when necessary. Does your involvement have anything to do with the police officer who was killed in prison?"

"Ex-police officer, and Parker and I did discuss Uris's death."

"Was not Mr. Uris accused of killing a young woman whom you later found hiding in North Carolina."

"Yes, Janis Bray, Nicholas Bray's daughter."

"Nicholas Bray, I met him once or twice."

Mr. Lewis did not elaborate, he didn't have to. So Bray had done business with the mob. Not a big deal, so had I. Then Mr. Lewis said, "Why don't we have a slice of that cheesecake now. You should wash your hands first."

I went into his bathroom, ran the tap, checked messages on my phone. When I came out, Mr. Louis was sitting at the table with the cheesecake. I noticed that his phone had been moved.

"We had no involvement in Mr. Uris's death," he said. Then we ate cheesecake and talked about The Untouchables – books, movies, and TV shows – until it was time for me to leave.

On my way home I called Parker, gave him Mr. Lewis's regards, and told him that Uris's death was not a mob-sanctioned hit. I did not tell him what I was going to do next. Being a thoroughly honest and decent man he would have objected.

I was not quite as honest and decent as Parker. Since what I was about to do was morally but not legally justified I decided to stay off the grid and worked off-duty and away from home, using the equivalent of a burner laptop my cyber-pirate friend Webster had lent me. I took the list of names from the FDC's full report and looked them up and tracked them down. Soon, with some help from Webster, I had their phone numbers, email addresses, and their financial and social media information. Then I started looking for that one slip.

It was one post from a man who barely had a social media presence. It read "It's done" and was posted by Correctional Supervisor Lee Kent the morning Morgan Uris died. Kent did not have that many listed followers but one of them was Herbert Morton, a former BPD Homicide Detective who had been appointed as an SAO investigator after either botching or covering up a homicide in which one of Alston's friends was involved. Damned fool liked the post. Well, Morton never was that smart.

I had never thought of Herb Morton as a crooked cop. His tanking of the murder case might have just been his natural laziness. But he might be the kind of cop who would do a "no questions asked" favor for a fellow officer and not see the tarnish such a favor put on his badge. It was time to find out.

I caught up with him the hallway of the Mitchell Courthouse. He had just picked up some subpoenae from Judge Kelly.

"Morton, can I have a couple of words?"

"Sure, Grace, what is it?"

"It's done."

Morton turned pale. "Wh-what do you mean?"

"It's just two words. I liked them, and so did you. My question to you is – who else did?"

"Grace, can we talk?"

"I know the perfect place."

The Homicide Unit. Parker's office. The Lieutenant started by reading Morton his rights "just in case." Morton has been a cop long enough to know when he was in a major jackpot and waived everything. Me, I just sat back and watched Parker work.

"I was just told to friend Lee Kent and pass along any posts from him that weren't bad jokes or funny animals. So when 'It's done' came across I passed it on."

"Did you pass on anything else?"

"Like what?"

"Like legal-sized envelopes filled with cash, a message to throw Uris to the wolves and put out the word he was a cop."

"LT, I would never …"

"Herb, listen to me. We can link Kent to putting Uris in the mix. I can link you to Kent. Now, as I have told many people many times, you're either a suspect or a witness. What's it going to be, Herb, a jail cell or the witness stand? And remember, the wrong answer might put *you* in the mix."

It didn't take Morton long to figure out which side he was on.

"Nothing like that. I was just asked to call Lee and give him a phone number, watch for his message, and report when I saw it."

"Why you?"

"Back in the day, we were sector partners."

"Who did the asking?"

Both Parker and I expected him to name one of the officers the task force was investigating. Instead he said,

"That tall, handsome guy from Alston's office … oh yeah, Manners."

Ogden Manners, Alston's second in command. Not that I've ever seen him command anything; he just does whatever she tells him.

Parker seldom swears. When he does it's usually because of something I did. But on hearing Ogden's name Parker let out a long, low whistle followed by a "Damn."

"She was behind it," Parker said quietly causing Morton to ask, "Ogden's a woman?" before figuring out who "She" was.

"And She's part of the task force," Parker went on. "So there's only one other reason She would be involved in something like this. She did it for Bray."

"Or Manners did it for Bray on his own," I suggested. "Maybe he got tired of taking orders from Alston for city money and wanted to move to a more lucrative position?"

My job was done. I had given Parker a viable lead that he was better able to follow than me. But something seemed off. Mr. Lewis had told me that Bray had connections. Connections that he could have used to take Uris out simply and quietly. This "Tinker to Evans to Chance" arrangement was just too complicated, too sloppy.

"Morton," I said, "Do you still have the number?"

"Yeah, Lee had me text it to him so he wouldn't forget it."

"Let's see your phone."

Morton got out his cell, laid it on the table. He showed us the text. With his phone on speaker, I called the number.

One ring, then another. It rang three more times before,

"Hi, you called me so you know who this is. Leave a message."

The first time I had heard that voice was in Holden Beach, North Carolina. The last time was in a small cemetery close to the open grave of Morgan Uris.

It seems like Janis Bray didn't believe in second chances either.

Lee Kent was arrested quietly later that day. Ogden Manners and Janis Bray's arrests were more public, he at his office, she at her Harbor East condo, both of them given the full perp walk in front of TV cameras and reporters from *The Sunpapers* and *The Baltimore Truth*.

I had given Alston a heads up and was with her when the news broke on local TV.

"He betrayed me and this office. Why?" There was sadness mixed with anger in her voice. Somewhere underneath that was the steel resolve that drove her.

"She used him. Made him think she was working for her father, that he could have the big money and a corner office." I turned my chair to face her. "He'll try to blame you. He'll say that he was only following your orders. Was he?"

"Damn you, Grace …"

"I don't think so. You'd rather have Uris as a living symbol of a bad cop than a man killed for having been a cop."

Alston had no answer for that. Instead, "You could have warned me, or didn't you want to?"

"You knew just after I did. Until we learned Manners was involved, Parker and I thought it was a cop targeted by your task force."

Then I hit her with my other news.

"I'm resigning, effective four weeks from now. I'll be taking three weeks' leave then come in the last week to finish things up. This is for you." I threw thick accordion folder on her desk.

"What's this?"

"It's you, Celina," my use of her first name got her full attention. "It's what been going in the State's Attorney's Office, your office — the Charm City Shred-It cover-up, the withholding of evidence in the Angel Collins/Officer Hays matter, the sweetheart plea you gave to Esslemont to hide your photos, the investigation or lack of one in the Judith Morrow murder, which brings us right back to Charm City Shred-It. This is your copy. I have a digital version all ready to send to Murphy of *The Baltimore Truth.* He'll love how you gave preferential treatment to The Brays when Janis disappeared and how that may have led to Manners going off the rails."

Whatever sadness had been in her voice was gone. There was nothing but steely anger when she asked, "Why show it to me? Why not send just it out?"

"I was going to. I was about to hit send and it would have felt so good to bring you down. But then I thought about the good you've done for this city in holding the police accountable. This …" I pointed to the folder. "… would undo all that, throw out the good with the bad. But from now on, you need to stick to the law and your crusade and stop using your job to run for mayor and bending the law for friends. That can only come back and hurt you and your mission. If you do, this folder stays between me and you."

"Why would you do that?"

"Everyone sinner deserves a second chance. I had mine, Morgan Uris wasted his, don't waste yours."

"And if I do?"

"I'll have a nice long talk with Murphy and drop you in the mix."

THE MAGNUM OPTION

I was finishing the last week of my four weeks' notice. Then it was goodbye State's Attorney's Office, a week on my own, then hello two weeks in Hawaii (at an Albion hotel of course) before taking on security duties at the Baltimore Albion, first training under Andre Henderson then running the show myself.

The Grand Jury wasted no time indicting Janis Bray, Ogden Manners, and Lee Kent for murder and conspiracy to commit murder. Nicholas Bray wasted no time in offering to testify about his dealings with organized crime in exchange for leniency for his daughter. Surprisingly, the mob did not kill him. Instead, information about his offshore accounts and his less than legal business transactions were leaked to the media and now he's facing enough federal indictments to keep him busy for quite some time.

To celebrate my resignation, Lieutenant Joshua Parker again took me to lunch at Mission BBQ. We ordered the same meals that we had the last time and as we finished, Parker said,

"I'm leaving Homicide."

"But you can't. You are Homicide."

"Not anymore. Remember Celina Alston's plan to start an Internal Affairs Division independent of the BPD?"

"You are the BPD."

"And I'll be the only one. I'll be looking for some good investigators, ones who are not themselves mean and who are neither tarnished nor afraid. You interested?"

At first, I didn't know what to say. Then, "Deacon, I'm honored. I'm also vindictive, afraid of a lot of things, and more than slightly tarnished."

"Doesn't matter. I know you're not Marlowe, although at times you think you are. I still want you working with me."

For a long couple of minutes I considered it. Then I thought of

Linda. When I first started working crime scenes, Parker scared the hell out of me. The thought of telling my wife that I was turning down working with her in favor of chasing bad cops scared me more than Parker ever had.

"Sorry, but I'm going into the hotel security business. But Linda got upper management to agree to let me run a small investigative agency out of my office as long as it doesn't interfere with my official duties. So if you need me, I've available at reasonable rates."

"So now you think you're Magnum but I'm glad to hear you say that, because I'm short-staffed and I've got some officers suspected of working a numbers' racket out of their patrol cars."

What the hell, I thought, *I have a week to kill.*

Biography

JOHN L. FRENCH is a retired crime scene supervisor with forty years' experience. He has seen more than his share of murders, shootings, and serious assaults. As a break from the realities of his job, he started writing science fiction, pulp, horror, fantasy, and, of course, crime fiction.

John's first story "Past Sins" was published in Hardboiled Magazine and was cited as one of the best Hardboiled stories of 1993. More crime fiction followed, appearing in Alfred Hitchcock's Mystery Magazine, the Fading Shadows magazines, and in collections by Barnes and Noble. Association with writers like James Chambers and the late, great C.J. Henderson led him to try horror fiction and to a still growing fascination with zombies and other undead things. His first horror story "The Right Solution" appeared in Marietta Publishing's *Lin Carter's Anton Zarnak*. Other horror stories followed in anthologies such as *The Dead Walk* and *Dark Furies*, both published by Die Monster Die books. It was in *Dark Furies* that his character Bianca Jones made her literary debut in "21 Doors," a story based on an old Baltimore legend and a creepy game his daughter used to play with her friends.

John's first book was *The Devil of Harbor City*, a novel done in the old pulp style. *Past Sins* and *Here There Be Monsters* followed. John was also consulting editor for Chelsea House's *Criminal Investigation* series. His other books include *The Assassins' Ball* (written with Patrick Thomas), *Souls on Fire, The Nightmare Strikes, Monsters Among Us, The Last Redhead, the Magic of Simon Tombs*, and *When the Moon Shines*. John is the editor of *To Hell in a Fast Car, Mermaids 13*, C. J. Henderson's *Challenge of the Unknown, Camelot 13* (with Patrick Thomas), and (with Greg Schauer) *With Great Power* ...

You can find John on Facebook or you can email him at him at jfrenchfam@aol.com.

Welcome to the Freakshow!

Monsters Among Us
a Bianca Jones collection

PAST SINS

Bad Cop. No Donu

THE GREY MONK
SOULS ON FIRE
JOHN L. FRENCH

J. L. ...CH

THE NIG MA STRI

"THE NIGHTM
-MICHAEL A.
OF CRIMES
AND THE EXECU
JOHN L. FREN

Welcome to Baltimore!

Here There Be MONSTERS
a Bianca Jones collection
JOHN L. FRENCH

IT'S A CRIME TO MISS THESE GREAT STORIES!

from author
John L. French

WWW.PADWOLF.COM

You can't get better than 13!

DOWN THESE MEANS STREETS

of Magic & Monsters walk the

MYSTIC INVESTIGATORS

"Patrick Thomas is... so believable it's unbelievable."
-Ida Vega-Landow, The Journal of the Lincoln Heights Literary Society
DEAD TO RITES
Patrick Thomas
C.J. Henderson
rites of passage
John L. French
Patrick Thomas
When Darkness Falls
The Department of
Mystic Affairs
Picks up the pieces
From The Murphy's Lore Universe of
PATRICK THOMAS
www.patthomas.net
Find us on Facebook!

Even the things that go Bump in the night
will learn that you DON'T mess with...
Terrorbelle
Fairy Rides the Lightning
Terrorbelle
PATRICK THOMAS
Fairy With A Gun
PATRICK THOMAS
"Thomas certainly brings the goods to the table
when it comes to writing urban fiction...I promise, you will love...
Terrorbelle: Fairy With a Gun. Who doesn't love a well-stacked,
ass-kicking, gun-toting, woman with bullet-proof, razor-sharp win
that investigates all manner of supernatural spookiness? I know
and Thomas's humor shows through in every tale. Jim Butcher an
Laurell K Hamilton have nothing on Thomas." The Raven's Barro
From The Murphy's Lore Universe of
PATRICK THOMAS

Terro
the Unco
PATRICK T

Shape up...
You only get
ONE Warning
Invocation
ONLY
Hex
PATRICK THOMAS
Darkness
CURSED
Hex marks the spot
PATRICK THOMAS

Hell's Detective
No One Is Above The
Even In
LORE & DYSORDER
PATRICK THOMAS
SHADOWS
PATRICK THOMAS
JOHN L. FRENCH
CASE OF THE MOON MANIAC
"Dark... and charming."
- Ellen Datlow,
The Best Horror of the Year Vol

One Last Chance to Save
Happily Ever After

...an a group of heroes including Goldenhair,
...ed Riding Hood and Rapunzel help General
...now White and her dwarven resistance
...ghters defeat the tyrannical Queen Cinderella?
...nd will they succeed before a war with
...Vonderland destroys everything?

...heir only hope to stop Cinderella's quest
...r power lies with a young girl named
...atience Muffet who carries the fabled
...hards of Cinderella's glass slippers.

...oy Mauritsen's fantasy adventure
...iry tale epic begins with *Shards*
Of The Glass Slipper: Queen Cinder.

**"Fantastic...
A Magnificent Epic!"**
-*Sarah Beth Durst* author of
Into The Wild & Drink, Slay, Love

**"The Brothers Grimm
meets
Lord Of The Rings!"**
-*Patrick Thomas,* author
of the *Murphy's Lore* series

**"Shards is a dark, lush,
full-throttle fantasy
epic that presents
a bold re-imagining
of classic characters."**
-David Wade, creator of
319 Dark Street

**"Roy Mauritsen's
enchanting epic
comes at a time
when fairy tales
are back in the
forefront of
our collective
imagination."**
-Darin Kennedy,
short fiction author

PADWOLF
PUBLISHING

In paperback & e-book
Find out more at:
shardsoftheglassslipper.com
padwolf.com"